Praise for *Recruits*

"Locke's newest novel has everything that readers love. Both intelligent and fast-paced, *Recruits* draws readers in quickly and holds their attention throughout. . . . This is definitely a must-read!"

—*RT Book Reviews*, 4½ stars

"*Recruits* is an accessible, clean science fiction novel ideal for those looking for titles with heart, thoughtfulness, and family values."

—*Foreword Reviews*

"*Recruits*, while outstanding, is a general market offering for those who enjoy science fiction. It's supposed to 'challenge young readers' understanding of time, space, and human limitations,' and it does so."

—*Christian MARKET* magazine

"Locke's imagination knows no bounds, and he successfully delivers a compelling tale of good versus evil and all the nuances in between."

—*Best Reads* blog

"*Recruits* by Thomas Locke is a fast-paced and engaging read that fans of science fiction and fantasy will love!"

—*Five Stars* blog

RENEGADES

Books by Thomas Locke

LEGENDS OF THE REALM

Emissary
Merchant of Alyss

FAULT LINES

Fault Lines
Trial Run
Flash Point

RECRUITS

Recruits
Renegades

RENEGADES

THOMAS LOCKE

Revell

a division of Baker Publishing Group
Grand Rapids, Michigan

© 2017 by T. Davis Bunn

Published by Revell
a division of Baker Publishing Group
PO Box 6287, Grand Rapids, MI 49516-6287
www.revellbooks.com

Printed in the United States of America

Library of Congress Cataloging-in-Publication Data is on file at the Library
of Congress, Washington, DC.

ISBN 978-0-8007-2790-1

17 18 19 20 21 22 23   7 6 5 4 3 2 1

I

The back roads of Virginia had always been Landon's best friend.

In the months after his father died, Landon had started escaping the world by driving out here. It was incredible just how empty the Virginia countryside could be. The world smelled sweet as the first dawn. Out here, he could pretend his mother wasn't hiding from life inside her prescription haze, that he wasn't suffocating in his community college classes, that he really could look forward to something better.

And finally, at long last, it did appear that he could. Look forward. Anticipate. Think of a future that was bigger than just getting by.

For one thing, his uncle, the senator, had offered him a gig as an intern. With pay, no less. Starting in eight days.

For another, he had been accepted at UVA. All his CC credits transferring. Scholarship. Not quite a full ride, but hey.

Landon had already given his notice to FedEx and was at

three days and counting. Then he was moving into his uncle's garage apartment, spending a summer in Georgetown, working the Hill, learning what it meant to breathe the heady air of Congress in emergency summer session.

There were two hours left to his eleven-hour shift. Landon had been at it since long before sunrise. Quick stops for breakfast at five thirty and lunch at eleven. His shoulders and neck and back were aching, but in a good way. He didn't even mind the grainy feel behind his eyeballs or the way the truck's cab was filled with the ripe smell of a long, hot day. Because he was saying goodbye. Not to the roads. He would always be coming back here. Hopefully someday to live. No, Landon Evans was saying farewell to somebody else's idea of a life.

Suddenly three people appeared out of nowhere, standing beside the road, looking straight at him. Then a strange-looking woman pointed something at his truck.

Two seconds later, Landon's motor died.

※※※

Sean Kirrel suffered through the most boring class ever.

Current Events and Future Trends. Each situation introduced by a list of wars and crises not even the planets involved still remembered. And taught by a professor named Kaviti. The name fit the guy perfectly. Kaviti was a pompous bore.

He paced across the front of the class as he droned, "Currently on the minds of the Assembly is Cygneus Prime. Its history is marred by almost constant strife, which they claim is now behind them. The leader of the largest fief on Cygneus Prime at the onset of the Second Interplanetary War was

Aldus, known to his loyal subjects as Aldus the Great and to his foes as the Butcher. Thirty-seven years ago, he defeated the last remaining opposition and established a governing council that rules the entire system, with one small exception known as the Outer Rim . . ."

Students at the Diplomatic Institute on Serena were called Attendants. Sean hated the word. It made him feel like a student in a school for glorified servants. Which, of course, was the intention. In truth, even Sean knew that much of his dissatisfaction had nothing to do with the school or his classes, and everything to do with Elenya. Their breakup had been eight months ago. His helplessness and her absence filled him with a restless pain that only heightened his dislike of this place.

"The latest Cygnean conflict began as a dispute over the mineral-rich world known as Aldwyn . . ."

Professor Kaviti was one of the most highly decorated members of the Diplomatic Corps. Not to mention a Justice in the Tribunal Courts and an alternate voting member to the Assembly Parliament. His second day in class, Sean decided Kaviti had suffocated his enemies with facts as dry as old bones.

Professor Kaviti liked to pick on Sean. And he was not alone. A segment of the faculty resented his presence. Sean had been sent here after less than sixty days as an initiate. Most Attendants arrived with five to ten years of Assembly schooling under their belts, then endured a rigorous examination process. In Sean's case, the Institute had been *ordered* to take him. By a planetary Ambassador and the founder of the Watcher school, no less. The fact that he and Dillon had saved an entire world from alien invasion only heightened this group's desire to find fault. There was no question in Sean's mind. Kaviti intended to down-check him and kick him out.

Kaviti's drone swam into the background as Sean picked at the open wound in his heart. He mentally replayed the argument from seven months ago, the last time he had managed to talk with Elenya. Actually, *talk* was probably not the right word to use. She had shouted, he had begged, she had left, end of story. She was gone now, off on some research assignment she would not discuss. Elenya had also told Sean not to come visit, which had pleased her mother to no end. The last time Sean had stopped by their home, the woman had actually smiled as she bade him farewell.

Sean was so lost in the misery of love gone bad he almost missed the Messenger's alert.

The first *bong* resonated through the classroom like a musical punch. After the second and third, Dillon popped into view. Which was almost comic, since Sean was pretty certain Dillon had no right to use the Messenger's calling card. Sean's twin brother was a cadet at the Academy, the military arm of the Human Assembly. The twins shared a contempt for the Messenger Corps. The Messenger's know-nothing existence was too close to the bureaucratic lifestyle that had framed their parents' world.

But Sean did not grin at his brother for two reasons. First, he would have gone into serious debt for any reason to leave Kaviti and his class behind.

The second was Dillon's expression. As grim as his uniform.

Dillon threw the teacher a parade-ground salute. "Apologies for the interruption, Ambassador. But Attendant Kirrel has been summoned."

"Summoned?" Another thing about Kaviti was his ability to dismiss with a sniff. It was claimed that, years after graduating, classmates of the Diplomatic school still greeted one another with an elongated snort. "By whom?"

"That is none of your concern, Ambassador. Sean?"

"See here! Just one minute, cadet!"

But Sean was already midway up the aisle. He asked his brother, "Where to?"

"Treehouse. Go."

"Already there," Sean replied. And he was. Bang and gone.

Dillon arrived an instant later. The air became compressed by his brother's tension.

Sean demanded, "What's the matter?"

"Landon Evans, remember him?"

"Sure. Carey's cousin."

"He's been kidnapped." Dillon pointed at Sean's closet. "Change into civvies. Jacket and tie. Hurry."

2

Two hundred and fourteen subalterns stood in silent ranks, waiting for the ceremony to begin. Above Logan's head, the brigade flag of his family's ancient enemy snapped in the wind. Logan kept a tight grip on the gilded staff, and an even fiercer one on his emotions.

So close. After so very, very long.

The parade ground formed the eastern segment of the battalion headquarters. The area was not a perfect square because a small river carved out one segment. Logan couldn't see the waters from where he stood. Directly in front of him rose a palace more than two thousand years old. Its origins were shrouded in myths. Supposedly Logan's clan had wrested the fief from dragons, then forced the beasts to carve the foundation stones and set them in place before allowing the remnants to descend into the inland sea that formed the province's eastern border. Such legends were officially banned by the council that now ruled Cygneus Prime. But the tales were still sung, usually late at night in roadside taverns that catered to the rebels.

Most of those once-proud warriors were gone now. Their ghosts stood in attendance inside an empty palace, courtiers to a father who had preferred death to the dishonor of life under new rulers. And so Logan and his mother had been left to fend for themselves in a land where they had no home.

Nowadays the old palace was only used for formal ceremonies like this, the annual parade of newly brevetted officers. The hall through which Logan had raced as a child stood empty, the old ghosts free to roam.

He allowed a spectral memory of his own to rise up—just one, but it was a fitting rebuke to the place and the day. When he was eight, he had stood very close to where he was now and watched as his father's body had been hung from the palace ramparts.

No doubt the ghosts of his ancestors were screaming in their vacant halls, appalled by the sight of the heir to the throne becoming an officer in the enemy's ranks. But Logan was at peace with himself and the deed. His father had made his choice and led a ragtag band to what he considered an honorable death. Logan's only legacy had been a childhood of hardship and misery.

From battalion headquarters at the parade ground's far corner, the officer of the watch tolled the changing of the guard. The bell sounded muted in the afternoon heat. Logan and his squadron had stood at attention for over an hour.

Then a trumpet sounded in the distance. Gradually the air became filled with a multitude of brassy instruments blaring away. If Logan had been a superstitious man, he might have declared it a warning against everything he had planned.

A bevy of air cars proceeded single file toward them. Logan shouted, as was his duty, "Officers, atten-*shun!*"

Two hundred and fourteen boots stomped the earth, and the two dozen officers supervising their graduation raised ceremonial blades to their chins. A multitude of air cars halted by the palace steps. Ranks of dignitaries alighted and climbed the stone stairs, followed by numerous proud families. The palace's terrace was decorated with bunting and rimmed by temporary bleachers. As the families found their seats, Logan watched the lovely daughter of an earl turn and give one of the subalterns behind him a discreet wave. A rush of indrawn laughter punctuated the ranks.

Logan's only friend in the platoon stood midway down the next-to-last row. Vance was a handsome rogue, despised by some for his boyish charm and carefree attitude. But the lower ranks adored him, for Vance was a born leader who laced most commands with an easy humor. Logan knew for a fact that he was also as brave as a dragon and immensely fierce in combat. Vance's talent with the ladies was legendary.

The ceremony took up most of the remaining day. Endless speeches were followed by a formal parade of troops, and then came the awarding of medals. Logan was the only subaltern to receive two, the gold brevet for best in class and the much rarer award for valor. He endured yet another speech before the second medal was pinned into place. He stood by the lectern, upon the stone plaza where he had played as a child, as the brigade's commander related how Logan had saved the lives of eleven fellow soldiers when the battalion had been ambushed during a supposedly routine border patrol. Vance was one of those who now owed Logan his life.

Then, finally, it was over. Logan trooped the regimental colors a final time, they received the dignitaries' salute, they cheered, and it was done.

Families streamed down the stairs and engulfed many of the newly brevetted officers. Vance sauntered over to where Logan stood on the perimeter and pretended to inspect his medals. "I don't suppose you could spare one of those baubles. Seeing as how you received two and I have none."

Logan gestured to the smiling young beauty who lingered on the middle step. "Pity they don't hand out medals for seduction. You'd have a chestful."

Vance squinted in her direction. "You know, I can't recall her name. How embarrassing. Be a good chap and introduce yourself, will you? She's bound to respond, and then I won't look like a total idiot."

"No time." Logan indicated the approaching officer. "We're on deck."

Vance gave the young woman a sorrowful wave. "What a waste."

"I need your help with what's coming next."

"Well, of course you do." Vance's grin outshone the sun. "Best friends and all that."

* * *

Logan and Vance entered battalion headquarters and returned the brigade commandant's salute. Logan's fellow officer

Nicolette stood in her subaltern's uniform by the commandant's desk and eyed Vance with genuine dislike.

The commandant served duty as the general's host that day. Clearly he disliked being relegated to a secondary position. The general's aide was there as well, a sour man named Gerrod, who said, "The general's invitation was for you alone, Logan."

"I respectfully ask that my two associates be included, sir," Logan replied. "They are essential to my plans."

"They are not your plans unless the general approves them."

"Aye, sir. Nonetheless, their assistance is crucial."

Gerrod was a bony individual with the taut-featured look of a man who had outgrown his own skin. His face was pocked from some old illness and his hair grew in tufts. But Logan had studied tactics under the man and knew the general had chosen wisely.

Gerrod said, "Wait here." He then said to the commandant, "The general will want their files."

When it was only the three of them and the duty officer, Nicolette said to Logan, "You can*not* be serious, including Vance."

Vance drew to ridiculous attention and threw a clown's salute. "A grand good afternoon to you as well, Officer Nicolette."

"You didn't say a *word* about him," she said to Logan.

"You're looking lovely as ever," Vance said.

"I *despise* you."

"Really? I've always found you rather fetching. In a stiff-necked sort of way."

"If he's going, I absolutely refuse—"

"Careful what you say," Logan warned. "Vance is vital. As are you."

"He's not to be trusted. He's despicable. He's a . . ."

"I believe the word you're looking for is *cad*," Vance offered cheerfully. "Of course, I did warn you."

Nicolette's response was a rude gesture that took Logan back to his childhood. His mother had done the same when especially angry with his father, such as the morning the man had ridden away for the very last time. "That is what I think of you," Nicolette said.

"Such a pity." Vance gave a mock sigh. "I've been head over heels since the very first time we—"

"Enough," Logan said. He turned his back to the grinning officer behind the duty desk. "It is decision time. Here are your choices. You can join with me and lead a squad each and make history. Or—"

"Rather a stark declaration for a newly brevetted subaltern to make," a voice behind them observed.

The duty officer jumped to his feet. "Atten-*shun!*"

General Brodwyn, the most highly decorated female warrior in the kingdom's long history, stepped forward and inspected Logan. She stood only a fraction shorter than him, and he was the tallest man in the room. Her grey gaze held a merciless and penetrating force, capable of peeling away his skull and studying his motives in precise detail. Logan had not been nervous until that very moment.

Finally she turned away, allowing his chest to unlock. "All of you, inside."

Sean found an exquisite pleasure in stripping off his grey Attendant uniform. The campus had an unwritten policy that all first-years were to wear nothing else, not even when off duty or back on their home world. Their identity was supposedly being reframed around the Human Assembly. But as Sean's home was an outpost world, such rules meant very little.

As he hung his outfit in the closet, Sean glanced at his brother. Dillon stood at parade rest in the exact place where he had arrived. The changes to his brother went a lot deeper than the battlefield-green uniform. These transformations had become much more evident since Dillon and Carey had broken up. On the rare occasions when the twins were together and off campus, Sean had the distinct impression that Dillon was intent upon leaving every vestige of his old life behind.

Sean took a quick shower, then selected clothes he had

not put on since Elenya stopped showing any interest in his home planet. She had shopped with him and picked the outfit back when things were good. Brooks Brothers grey slacks, black hounds-tooth jacket, starched white shirt, black loafers. Dillon filled him in as he dressed. Carey had been fitted with a signaling device that connected with whichever team of Watchers was assigned Earth duty. Twice she had tried to give it back, and Dillon had refused. The last time they met they argued over it. Dillon related the quarrel with a military-grade flat tone. As though the breakup had not shattered his existence.

Until recently, outpost worlds were scanned by Watchers only every few years. Which was how Dillon and Sean had not been identified until just before their eighteenth birthdays. But since then the alien enemies had changed tactics. They had targeted Sean and Dillon, the first-ever assault on an outpost world. Now there were Watchers on constant duty for every world that did not specifically forbid the Assembly's presence.

Sean asked, "Do I need a tie?"

"Probably a good idea, since you'll be meeting with the senator," Dillon replied.

Sean selected one of knitted silk, then returned to the loft's living area. Dillon stood between the dining table and the stairs, looking out the French doors to the balcony, the sunlit lawn, and the main house almost hidden beyond the summertime green.

Sean asked, "How long since you were back?"

"Six months. Longer. Not since Carey and I . . ." He

shrugged. "No reason to return and a lot of them to stay away. You?"

"Dinner with Carey and her dad. Couple of months, maybe longer." He inspected his brother. "Are you changing clothes?"

"No. I won't be going in."

"Okay."

"The uniform also serves as body armor."

"So . . . we're going after the bad guys."

Dillon gave him five seconds of tight focus. "You have a problem with that?"

Actually, Sean did. Not so much from the standpoint of doing what it took to bring Landon home. But Dillon's attitude troubled him at a deep level. "Anything more I should know going in?"

"No time." Dillon reached out his hand. "Grab hold."

They transited to the back garden of Senator Teddy Evans's Georgetown residence. Dillon remained behind the derelict shed and motioned Sean forward. "Find out what you can. When you're ready, I'll be here." He seated himself on a rusting lawn chair. "Go play diplomat. It's what you're good at."

The house and rear patio were fashioned from crumbling firebrick. Dillon had been here once for an awkward family gathering. The wife of Senator Evans was a Washington socialite who had put Dillon into a total snooze with her description of the home's history, how it had belonged to a signatory of the Constitution whose barges had plied the canal that framed the back garden. The house had been burned in the War of 1812, then rebuilt and expanded. Now it belonged to Senator Evans, his party's rising star and presidential hopeful.

Carey spotted Sean through the living room's French doors and rushed out to greet him. "Where's Dillon?"

"Sulking behind the shed."

She bit her lip and shook her head, but all she said was, "Come inside."

Sean heard an argument through the open doorway. "What's going on in there?"

Her response was cut off by the senator's wife. "Carey, how did your boyfriend get in our backyard?"

She kept a firm grip on Sean's hand, like she was afraid he'd bolt. "This is Dillon's brother, Sean."

"Oh, I'm sorry, you look just like . . ." The senator's wife rapped bloodred fingernails on the pearls strung around her neck. "Why ever didn't you use the front door?"

Carey's father, John Havilland, sat in a padded window box, partly hidden by the massive brick fireplace. He leapt to his feet at Sean's arrival and came rushing over. "Thank heavens. I was getting worried."

"I don't understand, John." The senator's wife wore so much hairspray it reflected the light. "What possible difference could this young man make?"

"Let's just say Sean and his brother have become experts at the impossible."

The living room swarmed with an alphabet of Washington security. FBI, police, Secret Service, even some bespectacled geek from NSA handling the phone tracking. Their gazes were laser tight on Sean, and they radiated a unified hostility. The senator with the boyish good looks rose from his position on the sofa. "That's just not good enough, John. I want to know what this fellow brings to the table."

"Maybe nothing." John led his daughter and Sean into the front hall. "Where's Dillon?"

"Out back."

"How absurd. Carey, go invite him in."

"Dad . . . please, no."

John grimaced at his daughter's response, but he merely asked Sean, "What do you need?"

"Privacy," Sean replied. "And something to eat. I missed a meal."

John led him to an upstairs bedroom. Carey brought a ready-made sandwich from the kitchen, and they took turns filling Sean in as he ate.

The details were sketchy at best. The handheld computers with which FedEx drivers scanned each package's bar code also updated their schedules. Drivers were required to code in between each drop-off and delivery. Landon had missed four different alerts, then failed to answer when the depot manager followed up by phone. Even so, the depot had been slow to become worried because of Landon's near-perfect record. Then Landon's shift ended with eleven pickups outstanding. When Landon still did not answer his phone, the Virginia state patrol was finally alerted.

Every FedEx truck was fitted with two GPS units. One was clearly visible when the hood was raised. This had apparently been located and destroyed. The second was hidden behind the gas tank. According to the FBI agent down-stairs, this second transponder was a closely held secret. The highway patrol had used this transponder to locate the truck on an isolated stretch of a Virginia county road. The door was open and the motor cold. Because Landon was over eighteen, officially the authorities were required to wait twenty-four hours before issuing a missing persons alert. But the depot manager was also Landon's friend, and he knew about Landon's famous uncle and the internship, so he called Washington. But by then the senator's security had been alerted.

Because the kidnappers had already phoned the senator's home.

The senator's wife had been warned that Landon would be killed if the police were brought in. But the senator had insisted, and now the place swarmed with them.

"We need to keep our voices down," John said. "Landon's mother is in the next room."

"Okay." If things went according to plan, Sean soon wouldn't be speaking at all.

"She's been put on heavy sedation."

"I understand." Sean had often heard about Carey's fa-vorite cousin. After Carey's own mother died, Landon had stayed close throughout the grieving process. Then Landon's mother started her soft descent into drug-addled isolation, and Carey had been there for him. Not daily, when she was living on the other side of the galaxy. But a lot.

Sean outlined what they needed, then sent Carey back downstairs. When his daughter left the room, John glanced at a photo of the senator and Carey's mother on the mantel and said, "The golden boy downstairs blames me for my wife's death."

"That's ridiculous."

"Of course it is. And they know it. But logic doesn't play any role here. Neither Teddy nor his wife thought I was right for her. They think if my wife had just listened, maybe somehow . . ." John shrugged miserably. "Family."

Sean nodded. Family.

"I worry that maybe all these past issues have left Carey unable to commit to her relationship with Dillon."

"No. That's not it." Sean could see John wanted to argue, so he went on, "Carey hated everything about the Academy."

"She called it a black lava prison," John recalled. "Even so, disliking a temporary residence is hardly reason—"

"Carey would have put up with it, no problem," Sean said. "She left because of the changes in Dillon."

"I saw Dillon less and less as time went on. All I had to go on was what Carey told me, which was not much, especially their last couple of months together." John had a professorial gaze, sharply intent and very intelligent. "The changes in him are so great?"

Sean did not want to discuss Dillon and his changes. The whole issue was very upsetting. And Sean had no one to talk with about his own breakup. The other students treated him as an unwelcome oddity. Most resented him and the attention he drew from every senior Assembly official who visited the Institute. Sean Kirrel was half of the twins who had vanquished the aliens. Who had saved a world and been decorated by the Assembly. And, if the rumors were true, who were also genuine Adepts.

John took Sean's silence as the answer he clearly expected and feared. He said, "Their breakup is tearing Carey apart."

Carey's footsteps could be heard racing up the stairs. She rushed into the room. "It's happening."

4

Logan had never been in the commandant's office before and was mildly disappointed to find nothing there of any interest. No battle flags, no warrior's gear, no tribute to past glories. It was as austere as the commandant himself, who retreated to the sofa in the far corner. General Brodwyn resumed her seat behind a desk as bare as the room save for three files. Two of the folders were quite thick, but the central one, the one that was open, held only a few meager pages. Logan felt his gut freeze at what he knew was coming next.

"Once every few years, a cadet wins both top honors," Brodwyn began. "It is customary for this cadet to be granted his or her preferred assignment. But before we discuss what this great quest of yours might be, I wish to know more about the young man I address."

Logan had feared this was would happen. He had spent sleepless nights debating how to respond. Now, in this instant, he still remained uncertain. "I don't like talking about my past, General."

"Nonetheless, I am ordering you to do just that."

Anything Logan said was a gamble. And he despised games of chance. He loved taking risks and wrenching a good result from bad odds. But only when he had control.

There was no certainty here, no control. His mind felt frozen with the tumble of unknowns. And yet, his gut told him to reveal the hidden truth.

Logan said, "I come from here, General."

He felt the rustle of surprise surround him. Only the general seemed at ease. "And yet you carry no hint of the local accent."

"I . . . My father died when I was very young. My mother and I moved to Radnor. I was raised in the capitol."

Brodwyn made a note on the top sheet of her file. "How did your father die?"

The tone was easy, a simple conversation between the two of them. But the way she avoided meeting his gaze, the hint of control beneath her smooth speech, was all the signal Logan required. He had done right to speak as he did. Because the general either already knew or suspected.

He said, "On a raid, General."

"So. Your father was a marauder. One who sought to drag your home province back into the endless war."

"Just so."

"His name?"

"He preferred to be known simply as the Count."

"So your grandfather . . ."

"Ruled this province until the Aldus invasion. I am the supposed heir of Hawk's Fief."

The suppressed tumult that filled the chamber left the general untouched. She repeated, "*Supposed* heir."

"Hawk's Fief is no more. All I have, all I am, is what I win for myself."

The commandant muttered, "Had I known this, I would never have granted him entry into officers' training."

"Then it is good that you did *not* know." The general had no need to raise her voice to silence him. Her gaze never left Logan. "I am curious. You feel no need to wreak vengeance on your victors?"

"Two thousand years ago, if the legends are to be believed, my forebears wrested these lands from an army of dragons. Our world's legacy is one of victors and the defeated. Hawk's Fief is no more. The title is dead. My father preferred myth to reality. There is no dishonor in calling him wrong."

She studied him for a time, then turned her attention to the two subalterns standing a pace behind Logan. "Were either of you aware of his past?"

"No, General."

"Not a hint, my lady."

"Why is that, I wonder?"

When Nicolette remained silent, Vance said, "I suspect Logan wanted to be judged on his own measure."

The general nodded her agreement, then turned back to Logan and said, "So you moved to the capitol."

"My mother sold herself into servitude with a merchant clan. I was allowed to study with their children."

The general added another note to her file. "Which explains your near-perfect scores on the entrance exams despite the absence of formal schooling."

"I was tutored." Logan recalled the beatings from two men who despised teaching one lowlier than themselves. *One day*, he swore silently. Then he realized the general still inspected him, and added feebly, "I studied very hard."

"Heir to a vanished throne becomes son of a slave. Then the servant's child is taught princely ways. You are indeed a rarity." She made another note. "Why the military? Surely the merchant's clan would have offered you a posting."

Because Logan was both ambitious and a fighter. Because he carried a lifetime of rage. Because the traders expected him to remain what he was in their eyes—a lesser mortal. Most of all, because of the secret Logan had hidden from everyone, even his mother, for seventeen long years.

He replied, "There is no other home for me, General. This is where I belong."

She leaned back. "I am satisfied with this young man's responses. I assume they carry sufficient merit to satisfy you as well, Commandant?"

"General, if I may—"

"Excellent. Very well, Logan. What position do you wish to apply for?"

He took the longest breath of his entire life. "I ask permission to establish a beachhead in the Outer Rim."

Logan managed to shock even the general. Yet he found no pleasure in this, for she could still refuse his request. And she had every reason to do so.

"You are aware," she said, "that our last effort to bring order to the Outer Rim ended in disaster."

"Yes, General. I am."

The general's aide, Gerrod, spoke for the first time since Logan had entered the room. "This is madness."

"On the surface, I agree." She turned to his two compatriots. "A marauder's son volunteers for an impossible duty. He brings with him two officers. One is the son of an earl—"

"Fourth son, if you will excuse the interruption, General." Vance's cheerfulness was spiced now with bitter ire. "And little good that does me. My eldest brother despises the ground I walk on."

"So the acquisition of a staff appointment . . ."

"Would certainly be possible, if my elder brother would spend the required gold. Which he will not."

She turned her attention to Nicolette. "And beside the earl's son stands the daughter of the district's chief of police. Does your father know of your volunteering for this operation?"

"He does, General. And he disapproves. But it is within my rights—"

"And it is within *my* rights to deny your request."

Nicolette struggled with the emotions that boiled to her face. "Don't. Please."

"A more unlikely trio I have never seen. And a more bizarre request . . ." She studied them in turn. "What makes you think you can succeed where far more seasoned troops failed miserably?"

That was one question Logan could not answer. Not yet. Not and survive.

Thankfully, Vance replied for him. "General, Logan has a plan."

Gerrod barked, "Our last attempt was led by one of our most seasoned officers. He lost an entire *battalion*."

Brodwyn said, "I assume you don't expect me to sacrifice hundreds more."

"All we want," Nicolette replied, "is a squad."

"All volunteers," Vance said, extracting a list from his pocket. "Here are their names."

The commandant had moved up to stand beside the aide. "You obviously failed to tell them of their chances."

"Which are nonexistent," the aide said.

"With respect, sirs, we disagree," Nicolette replied. "And to answer your question, Commandant, our volunteers are all aware of what happened to the battalion."

The general said, "So tell me this plan."

Logan had told his two officers everything. They were the first to know his secret, and trusting them had been the hardest act of a very difficult life. They had seen what it had cost him and responded as he had desperately hoped. They had demanded to see the secret for themselves. Then they had agreed to join him.

Vance and Nicolette showed this trust now, replying in turn, giving the general everything except the one item that made all the difference. Logan's secret.

The general rose from her chair and walked to the window. She listened to them with her back to the room. When they finished, she remained where she was. "I suppose there are special requests."

"Only three, General," Nicolette said. "First, no one outside this room is to know of our operation."

The commandant sputtered, "You can't possibly suggest there are spies—"

"The subaltern is wise beyond her years," Brodwyn said. "Next?"

"We need a space-going vessel assigned to us for the entire period."

"Fighter?"

"No, General. Transport."

Gerrod said, "No bombers? No backup troops? This is worse than absurd. It is suicidal."

The general spoke to the sunset. "And third?"

Logan was the one to reply. "General, I respectfully request that your aide, Adjutant Gerrod, serve as observer."

"Interesting. Explain."

"He expects us to fail. If we can convince him, we have an ally at the highest ranks of our military. And something more. You trust him with your secrets. We can therefore do the same."

The general began rocking back and forth, heel to toe. "There are elements to your plan that you are not sharing with me?"

Logan did not respond.

"I see." The hands clasped behind her back pointed at Vance and Nicolette. "So the two of you have no problems taking orders from . . ."

"The son of a licensed slave, the child of a scullery maid," Vance finished for her. "My dear brother the earl would be appalled at such a breach of etiquette. But that has nothing to do with our situation."

"No?"

"General, Logan happens to be the finest warrior I have ever known."

Nicolette added, "And we will not fail."

5

ean had not gone hunting in almost a year. The breakup
and resulting upheaval had restricted a lot of his abilities.
The same had happened to his brother. He and Dillon had
not managed to communicate at thought level for over nine
months. But there was nothing to be gained by worrying.
Either he could manage this or he couldn't. Sean's hope was
that the life-or-death situation Landon probably faced would
be enough to punch Sean through his emotional barriers.

He shielded himself, then compressed his awareness into
the core point just below his navel. He took a hard breath.
Then he extended.

The separation carried the familiar instant of near-death
terror, then he was out.

Hunting.

The bodiless pursuit had never come naturally to Sean.
Watchers learned this as a vital component of their duties.
Dillon was the first ever to have come up with this while still

an initiate. Even so, Dillon's current emotional crisis had cost him this ability as well. Another issue they did not discuss.

Sean turned his attention to the room below where his body lay and instantly sank through the bedroom floor.

The living room was filled with dense anxiety, an acrid stench Sean could almost smell with nostrils he no longer possessed. The only people seated now were the senator and the geek handling the tracking equipment. The senator's wife stood by the empty fireplace, twisting a linen handkerchief in her hands. A man in a sweat-stained shirt held up a small whiteboard to the senator, who said into the phone, "We need a proof of life."

The response played through speakers attached to the NSA geek's laptop. The voice was coppery from some kind of electronic disguise. "No questions, no deals, no cops."

The geek held up a whiteboard of his own that read, *50 seconds.*

The man standing near the senator had a gold badge and gun clipped to his belt. He used his stained sleeve to clear his board and scribble again. The senator read out loud, "We understand your request. We acknowledge—"

"Twenty million dollars. Have it ready by five. Any later, the kid loses a finger. Any radio tags or dye packets in the cash, the kid loses a hand. We even *smell* the cops, the kid comes back in pieces." The connection clicked off.

The geek peeled off his headphones and said, "Nothing. I got as far as a cutout in Vancouver."

One of the cops muttered, "None of this makes sense. Why go after a senator's nephew?"

"He's got a point," another said. "All this planning, why not a billionaire's son?"

"Because it's not about the money," the agent with the whiteboard said. He stepped to one side so the senator's wife could join her husband on the sofa. "The money is a test."

"That's good," the senator said. "Because we don't have twenty million dollars. Not even close."

Sean could hear every conversation in the room. Including that of the pair of grey-suited agents tucked just beyond the open door leading to the kitchen. He heard one of them mutter softly, "The senator doesn't have a clue."

The other said, "We need to alert the director."

"I already made the call. The director's on his way back from Utah. He's three and a half hours out. We're ordered to wait for his arrival."

"Three hours is too long," the first said. "You know what the next step is. Body parts."

His companion did not respond.

"You're CIA. This is your call. Call the attorney general or the chief of homeland. Somebody with the chops to prep the senator and his wife." He moved in closer and hissed, "The instant the kidnappers make a demand other than money, this becomes a threat to national security. The director won't be in charge anymore. This will be kicked up to a whole new level. You're just anticipating the inevitable."

"I don't know," the second man fretted.

"You want the senator and his wife to get the first delivery without any warning?" He jabbed the other man in the chest. "Make the call."

Sean knew he had stayed too long, but the next step frightened him. Even so, he knew there was nothing more to be gained here. He turned and took aim as best he could, naming his destination with all the intent of a man carving stone. Tracking the call.

* * *

One moment Sean was in a Georgetown parlor. The next, he hovered in the front yard of a derelict farmhouse. Two of the four front windows had cardboard taped over broken glass. Grey flakes of old paint littered the weed-strewn yard. Far in the distance, beyond a strand of stumpy pine, trucks rumbled along a two-lane highway. Directly in front of him stood a man and a woman. The man was dressed in what Sean instantly classed as terrorist chic. Black knit mock turtleneck and black gabardines tucked into black lace-up boots. The black canvas belt held four holsters for his Taser, phone, knife, and gun. Black wraparound shades. Olive skin and thick black hair swept straight back. Tall, slender, aloof, dangerous.

The kidnapper unplugged his cell phone from a tablet the woman held. Her appearance was the exact opposite of the man's—short, dumpy, multiple piercings, faded T-shirt, hiking sandals, orange socks, rust-colored hair cropped so short Sean could see her scalp.

She wound up the cable and stowed it in the pocket of her rumpled jeans. "We good?"

The kidnapper had a slight accent, but Sean could not place it. "You are certain my voice was not recognizable?"

"See for yourself." She swiveled the tablet around. "The synthesizer worked perfectly. And the call was routed all over the globe."

He continued to watch the distant traffic. "Go tell Bennie to prepare the first item."

"Bennie can get squeamish over stuff like this." She was already moving for the house. "I'll make the cut myself."

***

As soon as Sean opened his eyes, Carey spotted his alarm. "What's the matter?"

He swung his feet to the floor and sat up. The world spun so violently he thought he was going to be sick.

"Sean, what's—"

"No time." He stood too fast, sank back onto the bed, and groaned against the roller coaster behind his eyes.

John gripped his arm. "Can you walk?"

Walking was not the problem. Sean asked the professor, "Will you come with me?"

"Of course."

Sean used John's hand as support to stand and stay standing. "Step forward on three. One, two . . ."

Normally Sean needed a half hour or so to fully recover from a hunt. During those thirty minutes, he felt slightly disjointed, like he was still not knitted back together. He had never before transited immediately after. Shifting to the senator's backyard left him feeling awful.

Dillon, on the other hand, looked positively giddy with excitement, which was typical for him. Nothing got Dillon's motor running like the prospect of battle. He asked Sean, "You found Landon?"

"Yes. We have to hurry. They're going to cut Landon."

"I'll take it from here, John." Dillon replaced John's hand with his own. "Let's move."

Sean warned, "I'm going to hurl."

"Not on the uniform. They're a pain to clean. Okay, let's go."

Sean swallowed hard and said to John, "Stay here. I'll bring—"

"He's got it, Sean," Dillon said. "Let's *go.*"

6

They arrived at the exact same point Sean had been before. Same pale washed-out sky, same weedy yard, same old house. Only this time, no kidnappers were standing in the front yard.

Sean bent over and was sick. He held his position, hands gripping his thighs, until the world stopped spinning. When he was finally able to lift his head, Dillon was already approaching the house.

Sean tried to catch up on unsteady legs but tripped over a clump of weeds and fell flat on his face. He watched from the prone position as his brother kicked in the front door.

Sean Kirrel. The last guy you want watching your back in a fight.

He staggered up the stairs and entered a tightly enclosed battlefield. The dark-suited kidnapper stood in a doorway opposite the house's front entrance. He shouted as he fired.

Dillon's shield shimmered like water being struck by a fistful of rocks, but it held. Even so, the bullets' impact smashed Dillon back into the corner. His shield was coated with dust and plaster from shots that had gone wide. It was like Sean stared at a filthy grey ball.

Dillon yelled, "Find him!"

It was only when the kidnapper turned his way that Sean realized he had forgotten to shield himself.

The kidnapper's movements were smooth as falling liquid, a shift of his entire body, the two-handed grip flowing around until Sean stared straight into the barrel big as a cave, big as approaching death.

The only thing that saved him was the firing pin clicking on an empty chamber. The kidnapper cursed and slipped through the rear doorway.

The flash of near death erased Sean's nausea and dizziness, completely replacing them with an adrenaline rush. Which was a good thing, because the woman Sean had last seen in the front yard popped through the doorway. She held a short-barrel shotgun at waist level.

Sean had not practiced any attack methods since his early days, but it was good to know he had not forgotten his lessons. He connected with the energy core, shielded himself, then extended his arms. The woman saw his empty hands and must have assumed he was trying to surrender, because she smiled as she pulled the trigger.

Sean saw the blast of fire and heard the roar. Then he was knocked backward so hard he shot back through the doorway behind him and landed in the front yard. Again.

It was only when he leapt to his feet that he realized he had managed to get off a blast of his own.

His view through the front door was out the back of the house, through several walls that no longer existed.

"Sean!"

"Yeah!"

"You okay?"

"Totally." He climbed the front stairs and saw that his own attack had formed a trio of near-perfect circles. The door leading to the back room was gone. And most of the bathroom. Two waterspouts decorated the view of the backyard and the forest beyond. Just as Sean spotted the woman sprawled in the weeds, the lead kidnapper sprang through what was left of the door and took aim. Sean responded like he'd taken down armed bandits all his life. A mental flick of power, and the guy did a trapeze act out through yet another hole in the rear wall. Only with no net to stop his fall.

A third man spun through the wreckage, grimacing through a mask of dust and debris. Sean reinforced his shield and gripped what remained of the doorjamb.

Dillon said, "I got this."

The third kidnapper managed to get off one shot before Dillon lifted him ten inches off the floor and compressed him. The guy struggled like he was being fit into an invisible straitjacket. The arm holding the gun was smashed into his side. His legs kicked wildly, then made no motion at all. Dillon kept compressing the guy until he emitted tight little keening noises.

Dillon walked over, lowered him, picked up a knife from

the floor, and rapped the kidnapper hard in the forehead with the hilt. The guy went limp. Dillon let him fall to the ground.

Together Sean and Dillon entered the rear room to discover Landon Evans bound to a straight-backed chair with electrical tape around his chest and waist and legs. His left hand was strapped to a kitchen table. His terror mangled the words. "D-Dillon? W-what are you doing here?"

"Carey asked us to help." Dillon checked his hand, then told Sean, "Looks like we got here in time."

Landon leaked tears. "They were going to . . ."

"We know. But you're safe now." Dillon began working on the bonds. He said to Sean, "Find us some rope to tie up those dudes."

"Don't you have something more high-tech for that?"

"Absolutely." Dillon freed Landon's hand, then started on the chair. "Carbon and titanium. You got me?"

"Yes." Such items could not be left behind when they vanished.

Sean found a thick roll of silver electrician's tape beside what was left of the bathtub. He dried it off on his shirt, then carefully lowered himself to the ground. After he picked his way through the rubble, he used the tape to bind the kidnapper. The man coughed and tried to struggle, but his brain and limbs remained inside his barely conscious fog. Then Sean heard footsteps and wheeled about to discover the woman had risen from the weeds and was racing for the forest.

"Dillon, we've got a runner!"

Dillon appeared in the opening. "Okay, I got this." He lifted the woman from the earth. Her four limbs stretched out like she was playing starfish in midair. As he drew her back to where Sean stood over the kidnapper, Dillon pulled her limbs together, wrist to wrist to ankles. She remained poised about ten inches above the ground, like she was seated on an invisible stool, waiting for Sean to truss her up. Which he did.

When Sean had applied a final strip of tape over her mouth, he turned back and asked, "What do I do with them?"

"They'll keep right where they are." Dillon dropped to the ground and used his force to draw out the third kidnapper and deposit him beside the others. "Get that guy's phone."

The lead kidnapper's eyes could not have been any rounder and stayed inside his skull. Sean unclipped the phone from its pouch and carried it back. Dillon gave him a hand up into the house and said, "If we take Landon away from here, the kidnappers might walk free."

"I hadn't thought of that."

"Me either, until now." Dillon indicated the phone in Sean's hand. "Call the white hats."

Sean phoned Carey. When she answered, he said, "Landon's safe. Pass me over to the cops."

He listened to her stumble down the stairs, then breathlessly she asked, "He's really okay?"

"You'll see for yourself soon enough. Your dad still in the backyard?"

"Yes."

"Tell him to come back inside."

Carey stumbled through her thanks, then passed over the

phone. A voice raspy with exhaustion demanded, "Who is this?"

Sean returned Dillon's dusty grin and replied, "Track this phone. Landon Evans is safe and waiting for your pickup. The kidnappers will keep until you show up."

7

General Brodwyn's force of will was so strong she held her two officers to silence, though both the commandant and her own adjutant quivered with outrage over her seriously considering Logan's request. Logan had no idea how long they stood there, he and Nicolette and Vance still at attention before the now-empty desk. Time slowed to where each beat of his heart seemed thunderously long. His life, his future, rested in the balance. And all he could do was wait.

When she spoke, it was to the gathering twilight beyond the window. "I give you three weeks."

Logan's relief was so strong he could scarcely breathe. Thankfully, Nicolette answered for him. "That is not enough, General."

"Nonetheless, it is all you shall have. I gave my friend six weeks, and now I have the blood of five hundred troops on my hands, and my friend is permanently absent."

Her aide said, "General, I must object in the strongest possible—"

"Three weeks. Starting now. Not one instant longer. Gerrod, you are to observe. And you will do so from your office. No off-planet sorties unless I give you a direct order." Her breath continued to fog the window. "Perhaps the shortened time span will save your company, Logan. But I doubt it."

The commandant said, "General, this is a totally futile—"

"Commandant, are you aware that an inspectorate from the Human Assembly is arriving on Cygneus Prime?"

"I . . . What?"

"One condition for our entrance into the Assembly is, we must make every effort to protect our citizens."

Logan had never before met the camp commandant. The closest he had come to the man had been holding the brigade's standard on parade. But Logan knew what others thought of him. The commandant was a precise man who liked numbers more than men and planning far more than action. He was probably ideal as the leader of a training camp well removed from battle.

The commandant fumbled his response. "General . . . I don't see . . ."

"Precisely. What possible good could this ragtag band do? The answer most certainly is, none whatsoever. But that is not the point." Brodwyn returned to her place behind the desk. "Our ruling council ordered me to bring the Outer Rim under control. Our army failed. Our *army*, Commandant. They *failed*. So I ask you. What possible answer can we offer the inspectorate when they arrive?"

When the commandant did not respond, Vance offered, "That we have continued to try."

"Exactly. But the minister of defense, my direct superior, did not gain his position by sacrificing good men on futile gestures." She pointed to Nicolette. "Do you understand why I am divulging state secrets?"

Nicolette nodded. "Because you think—"

"I do not *think*, soldier. I *know*."

"—you're sending us on a suicide mission."

Brodwyn let the silence own them for a time. "Well?"

Nicolette's voice did not waver. "Asked and answered, General. We will not fail."

ean returned to Georgetown alone. He waited in a café a block away from the senator's home. An hour and a half later, confirmation arrived of Landon's safe retrieval and the kidnappers' arrest. Sean's rewards were a hug from Carey and a handshake from John, which was far more than Dillon received.

Sean transited to the Institute just as the apprentice Diplomats filed into the dining hall. The student center had long, cafeteria-style tables where most Attendants were expected to take communal meals. This was another of the relentless rules — start practicing diplomacy through interaction with classmates. Senior instructors were on constant patrol via cameras that flitted about the public rooms. Enough downchecks and students spent years inside windowless vaults, sorting planetary archives. But after returning that evening he had no interest in company, no matter how many downchecks he earned.

He selected his food and headed for a table by the window where he could be alone. Some students came from worlds where certain meals required solitude. He decided that was what he would say if asked—the primitive culture on his outpost world demanded that he be alone. But no one approached. He watched the courtyard fountain through the window to his right and did his best to ignore the stares from other students that were reflected in the glass.

His meal finished, he pushed the tray to one side, opened his tablet, and began studying the lesson he had missed. Sean was certain Kaviti would pounce on him the next day. Soon he was lost in the convoluted mess that formed the political status of Cygneus Prime. Their politics actually made for a fascinating read. After centuries of rejecting the invitation, Cygneus had recently requested to join the Assembly.

Still today, the nine inhabited Cygnean planets were ruled by hereditary fiefs, with warrior tribes and liege lords and a whole host of menacing despots. According to some reports, a few deposed rulers had actually taken their entire populations into space, from where they preyed on the weak and sought to defeat their ancient foes.

"How's the food here?"

Sean looked up to see his brother standing next to the table. "Better than at Josef's school," he replied. "Marginally."

Dillon had changed into another uniform of cadet green. "You think anybody will object if I loaded up a tray?"

"Why don't you go see?"

Dillon sped through the line and returned with enough food for three people. "What are you studying?"

"Cygneus Prime."

Dillon ate at a ravenous pace. "Space pirates, right?"

"Give the guy a medal." Sean watched his brother wolf down the meal. "Work up an appetite, did we?"

"Bad habit," he said between bites. "I just finished twenty days of battlefield training. We only got a few minutes to eat."

Sean stowed his tablet and waited for Dillon to finish. Then he said, "This isn't just a friendly visit."

Dillon pushed his tray aside. "Nope."

"I'm thinking you came to warn me there might be some blowback."

Dillon wiped his mouth, then balled his napkin tighter and tighter. "I could have been wrong, involving you in this."

"Hey, we're a team."

"You may not feel that way once they start blasting away."

"Dillon, that gig was the first serious fun I've had in months."

His brother showed him the schoolyard grin. "For real?"

Sean's response was cut off by a Messenger bong, the loudest he had ever heard.

Dillon pushed back his chair. "Stand up."

The second chime carried enough force to compress Sean's chest. *Bong.* The third was louder still. *BONG.* Three Messengers appeared before them. At least, Sean assumed they were Messengers. But their uniforms were an electric blue. And in their hands were . . .

"Dillon Kirrel, Sean Kirrel, by the authority of the Human Assembly, I am hereby placing you under arrest."

Sean had heard about the devices the guards carried. They

looked like black steel cuffs. Clamps. They formed the worst of the student's tales, the ones that were whispered about late at night. They anchored the wearer and temporarily erased the power of transit.

Sean fought down nausea for the second time that day.

The guard stated, "If you attempt flight, the tribunal will take this as an admission of guilt."

"We're not going anywhere," Dillon said.

"The act of fleeing will be taken as a presumption of guilt. Your punishment will be set at the most extreme level allowed by law."

"This is us not running," Dillon said.

The guard stepped forward and gripped Sean's arm with the finality of a prison door. "Come with us."

9

Thirty-three hours after their meeting with General Brodwyn, Logan's team departed for the Outer Rim.

Their preparations became a madcap adventure all their own. No matter how fast Logan moved, the clock still beat him ragged. For all the orders he and Vance and Nicolette shouted, a hundred things were left undone. None of them slept. There was no time for a decent meal, hardly enough for a long breath.

From a distance, their ship looked like any number of free traders that plied the empty reaches. Up close it looked even worse, with pockmarked sides and a rusting undercarriage that seemed barely able to support its weight. Most of the vast interior was given over to the cargo that Logan hoped would pave their entry. The cramped chambers assigned to his team stank of long use and too many previous occupants. This was as it should be, for a most profitable outbound cargo was men. Aldwyn consumed miners at a voracious pace. Even so, the few who survived usually came home rich. There were always more willing to accept the hazards and near-certain death.

The ship's true value was hidden deep, for at its heart burned a ditrinium engine. A ditrinium motor transformed a ship, even one as nasty and battered as this, into a sleek jungle beast. This was one reason why the rare metal was so highly valued. The military-grade engine granted their vessel five times the legs of any standard transport and could outrun all but the swiftest fighters. As far as Logan was concerned, having the general assign him this vessel was Brodwyn's way of saying "good hunting."

Aldwyn was completely out of sync with the Cygnean system's other worlds. The rogue planet swam in an elliptical orbit. The farthest point of its nine-year cycle lay beyond the twin gas giants. Then it swung back inside all but the two worlds closest to their sun. Some said the months of endless dark drove everyone except the strongest mad.

Aldwyn was now approaching Cygneus on the inward swing. This meant most Cygnean ports were clogged with ships and men. But not theirs. At Logan's request, Brodwyn assigned them to the remotest military base with its own private landing site. The Outer Rim had spies of its own, and Logan could not risk word reaching Aldwyn of their approach.

Their base stood on an island just outside their planet's arctic circle. Even in the middle of summer the temperature remained frigid. There was neither snow nor ice, however, because the confluence of ocean currents kept all storms at bay. The island held one small village, nestled inside a rock-walled harbor. Otherwise the landscape was scrub and migrating birds and misery. But the ocean currents formed the richest fishing territory on Cygneus.

Nicolette stepped up beside Logan, who stood on the transport's rear deck, scowling at the windswept landing strip. "Something the matter?"

"I know I've forgotten something."

"You're exhausted. We all are." She glanced back at where the two squads were finishing their first hot meal in two days. "They did an amazing job."

"When we're a million miles out and it's too late, I'll realize what it is I've left undone."

"That's the sign of a good leader, worrying," Nicolette replied. "Where's Vance?"

"Coming."

She snorted. "If he's late, you should make this place his next assignment."

"Vance is never late."

"He deserves this place. He can spend his days romancing the gulls." She squinted against a blast of frigid wind. "And the eels. They're made for each other."

Logan pointed into the gloom. "Here he comes now."

"Pity, that."

"Nicolette . . ."

"I told you I'll work with him and I will. But I don't have to like it."

When the base transport halted before the ship's loading platform, Logan realized Vance was so hungover as to appear near death. Two grinning squaddies stepped down, then gently lifted Vance from the rear seat. The subaltern squinted against the half-light. The soldiers gripped his arms and half dragged, half carried him into the hold.

Nicolette greeted him with, "You truly are disgusting."

"Softly, softly," Vance moaned. "You are in the company of the sorely afflicted."

"How did you find the time? How did you find the drink?"

"Don't forget the ladies," one of the soldiers added. "Three of them."

Vance winced as the ship sounded its alarm and the portal rumbled shut. "Deposit me in some dark corner, that's a good lad," he said.

Logan pointed the soldiers toward the officers' quarters, then said to Nicolette, "Inform the pilots we are good to go."

⁂

The captain was named Hattie. She and her six-man crew only entered the hold twice during the five-day voyage. Both times they were taciturn to the point of rudeness. Logan found no fault in their attitude. Hattie flew a small bevy of troops to what she assumed was certain death. Neither she nor her crew had any interest in getting to know soldiers who would soon become corpses.

The steel hatch between the hold and the control room remained locked from the other side. Their isolation suited Logan perfectly. He spent the entire journey preparing his team.

Until that point, only Vance and Nicolette knew what he

had in mind, and for them it was all theory. They had come with him primarily on trust. Now they saw the truth revealed.

It all came down to the secret Logan had carried since childhood. Three days after his ninth birthday, he had developed an enhanced awareness. He called it a new sense of smell.

He had no other way to describe the change. His nostrils played no part, and yet he smelled a difference in one of his friends. They were all scavengers who flitted from shadow to shadow within the capitol's winding ways. Poverty-stricken and always hungry, they clustered together for survival. Logan had not much cared for many of them. But affection played less of a role than the need for combined strength.

One of his favorite friends had been the first new scent he had detected, a rat-faced girl who at first had no idea what he was talking about when he said she could move from place to place without walking. He did not think this. He *knew*. Just as he knew that this was a secret he could share with no one. The legends of the ghost-walkers and the Assassins formed their favorite childhood game. Ghost-walkers could travel in an instant, they threatened the fabric of reality and fiefdoms, the Assassins wiped them out. They had not existed within the Cygnean system for over a thousand years. Only Logan and his scrawny friend knew different.

Then he smelled a second. And a third. And three more. By then, seven years had passed. Logan was old enough to think and to plan.

They broke off all contact with the others and formed a new gang. Logan continued to find others. He came upon them in the alleys and the gutters. He had to find them young, before the harsh life quenched the soul's fragile flames. They had to be able to listen, to obey, to bond. Older than eleven or twelve and they were feral beasts in human skin, good for nothing but trouble. And that was the one thing Logan knew they had to avoid. Their survival depended upon going unseen, which required discipline.

Discipline was what drew him into the military. He needed to learn how to lead by following. He needed to find a place where they might forge a bond and survive beyond the next theft. For they were all stealing now, taking what they needed in order to survive. Never too much, and never from the same place twice. Despite his best efforts, however, rumors had begun surfacing that ghost-walkers were about. Logan heard about secret police who were ordered to kill on sight. He knew their time was running out.

The only way they could survive was by proving their worth. Doing the impossible. Succeeding because of their secret gift. Swearing allegiance to a leader strong enough to keep them alive.

When they lifted off from the island keep, Logan's team numbered nineteen.

Nineteen civilian ghost-walkers, thirty unseasoned troops, and three officers. Hardly a force to be reckoned with.

Which was precisely what Logan had in mind. He would enter an impossible situation against insurmountable odds and give his leaders a victory they had never imagined possible.

Then again, they might all die. The risk was both real and almost likely. But Logan had lived with deadly secrets for so long, he could find a faint peace in doing his best and not succeeding. So many lives he had known were wasted upon the next drink, the next wench, the feeble excuse of pleasures that came hard and left easy. At least he and his team would give their all for a reason greater than just another forlorn hour.

They trained hard. Logan and his two officers explained the plan through practice. They introduced the wide-eyed squad of regular troops to the concept of being transported instantly from one hold to the next. Back and forth, fashioning teams of three and four, creating a flexible pattern that could be redesigned to suit whatever terrain or threat they encountered. Working on speed and stealth and silent attack. Hour after grueling hour. Logan was never satisfied, but he praised them just the same. And then sent them back to do it all again. Only Vance refused to be transported. He observed, he commanded well, but he held back. Logan did not insist. Nor did he allow Nicolette to mock Vance.

Four days after liftoff, Logan arranged a feast. He invited the pilots and was glad when they declined. The ship carried a wealth of fresh produce, and the meal was splendid. When they had all eaten their fill and the songs had been sung and the peace was strong between them, he rose to his feet and called for silence.

They were a motley crew, the civilians streetwise and scrawny and feral and squinty-eyed. The squaddies who had volunteered for this duty were mostly dross as well. They were the leftovers no one wanted, but because they had managed to scrape by in basic training, they were called soldiers. Theirs was a feeble future of clerking and following someone else's orders, years of shelving boots and classing uniforms and preparing supplies for those who went off to fight. But the same desperate need radiated from all their faces. They were soldiers because they belonged nowhere else, and because of this they were superior to almost everyone in Logan's eyes.

"When I was very young, my father sang me to sleep," he began. "It is the only clear memory I have of the man, other than watching him swing from the palace ramparts after they hung him for being the marauder he was. He sang to me the outlaw tunes, the legends that fashioned the earliest memories of my clan. The Hawks were known as the fiercest of warriors. But their time of true glory was long ago. The Hawks I knew were a defeated lot who fed themselves more on myth than reality. But I have studied our race's history, and I know that at least some of the legends are borne on truth. Our world was once ruled by dragons."

He began pacing back and forth. "The finest tales, the ones I loved hearing most, were about the heroes who defeated the dragons and claimed this world for humankind. Nowadays our leaders have ordered that the legends be erased from memory. But the family that enslaved my mother traded secretly in the ancient scrolls. I read all I could find, and I tell you the ghost-walkers were how the dragons were finally defeated. After that final battle, clan leaders who feared the ghost-walkers' power sent out Assassins to eradicate them and all their families. And so they vanished. Never to be seen again."

Logan turned to face his crew. "Until now."

He let the words hang in the air, then began pacing once

more. "The dragons were feared for their size and their ferocity, but even worse was how they had the ability to spout death. Some shot an unseen fire so fierce it melted the thickest armor, others an invisible poison that ate the bones of men. But most dread of all were the beasts that breathed a potion of pure, distilled fear that turned the stoutest hearts to vessels of terror.

"When the ghost-walkers became soldiers and were sent out to do battle with the beasts and their lords, they took this dread weapon as their name. The walkers became known as Dragon's Breath. And that is the title I give to us today. We are the invisible bringers of doom to all who stand in our way."

Logan stopped and waited.

Vance snarled, "Troops, atten-*shun*!"

If anything, Nicolette's command was fiercer still. "Dragon's Breath, salute!"

10

The prison where Sean and Dillon were kept wasn't so bad, as far as prisons went.

The Human Assembly's central government occupied a peninsula that extended like a giant thumb from Serena's largest continent. Every student and cadet knew about the prison. The place held a horrid fascination. Cliffs at the peninsula's eastern tip were carved into thirty-three levels. The upper floors held the Justice Tribunal records and the offices of Messenger guards on prison detail. Below that stretched the disciplinary compound.

Each floor of the prison was built around a large central commons area. So long as inmates behaved, they were permitted the run of their level. But all the doors were steel, and all the locks were on the other side.

Sean and Dillon both spent the first two days in their bunks. They met for meals, and Dillon apologized repeatedly for getting Sean involved. After the first few times,

Sean stopped responding. He hated where he was, but the isolation granted him the first chance he'd had in months to freely examine his life. And the truth was, he loathed most aspects of it.

Before, he'd blamed his misery on Elenya. But he now came to accept that his problems ran much deeper. Sean genuinely detested the school where he'd been assigned. Kaviti was only the worst of a bad lot. The teachers were pompous, old, and set in their ways. They never said it, but Sean knew they thought being transiters granted them superiority over lesser mortals. He hated how the students adopted the professors' attitude.

By the end of his second day in the prison, Sean had pretty much decided that even if he and Dillon somehow managed to leave with clean records, he was not going back to the Academy.

All the inmates on their level wore ankle clamps, making transiting impossible. He and Dillon were left entirely alone. At first Sean assumed the inmates were simply taking stock of the newcomers. But two days passed and no one spoke to them or even looked their way in the commons areas. Sean knew something bigger was at work. But Dillon seemed to remain intentionally blind to the exclusion, so Sean followed suit.

On the third day Sean emerged from his cell to discover Dillon working out in the central hold. His practiced moves were like karate but different. Sean watched for a while, marveling at his brother's new talent. Then he walked over and asked, "Can you teach me?"

Dillon took his time inspecting Sean. "Are you sure you want to?"

"Absolutely."

"Okay, for starters, stand up straight."

"I am."

"Look at me. Head up, shoulders back, stomach in. Better. Now balance forward. No, no, you're not going to dive out the window. Just a touch of pressure on the balls of your feet. Like a cat. Okay. Now follow my lead."

The practice was a bit of karate, a bit of jujitsu, and some totally off-the-wall, transit-based concepts thrown in for good measure. Dillon said the Academy simply referred to it as core combat.

Sean kept himself in fairly good shape, running or cycling or swimming almost every day. But after an hour and a half of following Dillon's lead, he was as exhausted as he had ever been in his entire life.

That night, Sean woke up every time he shifted position. The ache in his muscles and his joints was awful.

The next day was pure agony. But Dillon ignored his groans and kept him moving.

They worked out for three hours in the morning, broke for lunch, then were at it for four more hours in the afternoon. Long sessions of stretching, breathing routines, balance, endurance. Then Dillon moved on to tactics for strike and defense.

Hard as the routines were, Sean loved the hours spent bonding with his brother again. He relished the showers at the end of the day. He enjoyed seeing how Dillon was becoming a leader in his own right, teaching in a quiet, calm way, challenging Sean politely. Dillon's rough edges were becoming smoothed over, honed into a warrior's ability to show bravery even when caged for doing the right thing.

What Dillon taught by example was the most important lesson of all. Clamping down on fear and rage and frustration. Channeling the emotions, holding them firmly in place, never allowing them to dominate. Sean was learning the unspoken warrior's creed, and it drew him close to Dillon for the first time in over a year.

＊＊＊

The person who finally came to see them was a petite brunette who might have been beautiful had her expression not been so severe. She wore the grey-blue uniform of the high courts with a small gold starburst on her collar. Her short, dark hair spun like raven flax with every motion.

"I am Advocate Cylian. You may refer to me as Advocate or ma'am. I am here to represent you."

Sean had witnessed a few other conversations between Advocates and prisoners. Most of the time, inmates were ushered into a glass-walled cage where they spoke to officials through screens embedded in the wall. Today, however, a pair of Messenger guards positioned themselves well back, far enough away not to overhear but close enough to rush forward in the event of trouble. Sean had not seen any other Advocate arrive with protection.

He pointed to Cylian's escort and asked, "Why are they here?"

She ignored the question and led them to a table removed from all other prisoners. When Sean and Dillon were seated across from her, Cylian said, "The charges against you are extremely serious. I strongly advise you to throw yourself on the mercy of the court."

Sean glanced at his brother. Dillon gave a tight jerk of his chin, the signal they had used since childhood, acknowledging that Sean was on point.

Sean turned back to the Advocate and said, "Answer my question."

"The guards are not important. You need to focus on the issue at hand." Her face showed no emotion whatsoever. She might have been located a million miles away. "The crimes leveled against you carry a potential penalty of fifteen years' internment. Our strategy should be to avoid this if possible. However, I cannot—"

"The crimes," Sean repeated.

"Correct. If you—"

"I want to ask some questions. Clarify a couple of points. Since we're the ones accused here, I need to understand before we move forward."

The Advocate showed no reaction. Her face was bland as a Kabuki mask. "Ask your question, if you must."

"Questions," Sean corrected. "For instance, we've been held here for six days without anyone telling us what we're being accused of. I seem to recall reading for one of my classes that an Assembly prisoner must be charged at the time of imprisonment."

"There are extenuating circumstances in your case."

"Like what?"

"They are very complicated. For the moment, you need to focus on your response to the charges. You face the tribune tomorrow."

Sean's gut said that the woman was intentionally avoiding addressing his issues. As though she had come here with the aim of shepherding them.

Dillon remained silent, watchful. Trusting his twin totally. Ready to guard his back and strike where Sean pointed. Sean liked how they were fitting back into the mold that had seen them through any number of early battles.

As though in confirmation of his suspicions, the woman said, "Back to the charges." She started ticking them off on her fingers. "Unlawful use of the Messenger alert. Possession of a planetary Watcher signal by an outpost civilian. Unlawful use of said device. Application of transit forces on outpost world without prior permission. Fraudulent claim of official Assembly business by an Academy cadet. And the most serious of all, unlawful use of military force on an outpost world, witnessed by civilians of said planet."

Sean was only partly aware of her words. His initial sense that they were being railroaded escalated to certainty.

Cylian dropped her hands to the table. "Most of these are crimes punishable by imprisonment. Again, I strongly advise you to throw yourself on the mercy of the tribunal."

Sean said, "You want us to plead guilty."

"Precisely. You'll spend a couple of years clamped and assigned clerk duty. Your records will carry a down-check. But this would be balanced by your actions in the Lothian crisis."

"Back to my questions."

She shook her head. "Asked and answered. There is no time for nonessentials."

"But see, this is essential to us."

Her only response was to tap one finger on the table. Her nail was clipped short and polished with clear enamel.

Sean said, "You've come in here assuming we're guilty."

"Because you *are* guilty. The evidence is irrefutable."

Sean decided not to argue the point. "Did you volunteer for this case, or were you assigned?"

The finger tapped once, twice. "I hardly see—"

Dillon spoke for the first time since they had sat down. "Answer his question."

Cylian kept her gaze on Sean. "I was requested to take this assignment. I accepted."

"Who did the asking?"

"The senior Justice assigned to your tribunal."

"Who is that?"

"Really, this is hardly—" She stopped speaking because Dillon shifted forward until he looked ready to launch himself across the table. The two guards stepped toward them, then halted when she lifted her hand. "If you must know, it was Ambassador Kaviti."

Sean felt all the pieces swoop into place. He actually smiled.

Dillon asked, "He's your prof, right?"

"Yes." Sean asked Cylian, "You're on his staff, aren't you?"

She cocked her head, as though needing to examine him from a different perspective. "I am."

Dillon settled back into his seat. "This just keeps getting better."

"Actually," Sean said, "it does."

Cylian asked, "Can we return to the matter at hand?"

"We never left it," he replied. "It's nice of you to visit, but we won't be needing your services."

The Advocate's response surprised Sean. He had expected her to show outrage. Be offended. Instead, a tiny flicker of something else sparked in her dark gaze. There and gone in an instant. "Are you certain?"

Dillon said, "Thanks for stopping by."

She rose from the table, her gaze tightly focused on Sean. "I hope you know what you're doing."

Dillon waited until she and the guards had departed to ask, "Do you?"

11

ogan's teams maintained a watch-on-watch schedule throughout the voyage, though there was nothing to guard and no enemy within reach. But the duties were important, and that night Vance and Nicolette volunteered to stand a double watch together. Logan had no interest in returning to his steel chamber or in worrying through his last hours on this vessel. So he hunkered down in the main hold, back where no one would notice, and pretended to study the Aldwyn maps. All their charts were vague when it came to the Outer Rim. Logan filled the empty reaches with his worries.

He heard soft voices, and the tone surprised him. His two officers had snapped and quarreled for the entire journey. Until this moment, when he heard Nicolette say, "I should not have condemned you for what is your nature."

Logan heard their footsteps come closer, then halt just

beyond his alcove. He held his breath, intent on not allowing his presence to disturb their conversation.

"You are a stronger person than I will ever be," Vance replied.

Nicolette asked, "What brought that on?"

"I have wanted to apologize since the day we met in the commandant's office. I was wrong to treat you as I did. You are far too good to be anyone's plaything."

"Most women are," she said.

"You will forgive me if I speak only of you. To include all womankind would . . ."

"Leave you bereft and your life empty of purpose?"

"Something like that," Vance said. "I think in part I went after you like I did . . ."

"And then cast me aside like an empty plate," Nicolette added, but the bitterness for once was absent. "Like a meal enjoyed and then forgotten."

"All that," Vance said. "I knew you were better than me. I knew . . ."

Logan's left leg itched so fiercely it trembled. He felt an overpowering urge to sneeze. He stifled both as best he could and did not move.

"My family comes from the mountain fastness east of the capitol," Nicolette said. "My forebears were clan leaders whose lands were swallowed by the Aldeans."

"Like Logan's clan, the Hawk Fief," Vance said, the surprise clear in his voice.

"Only our defeat was done in gentlemanly fashion. The Aldean warriors surrounded our lands. They invited my great-grandfather to join them in an alliance, which was a polite way of saying that either he agreed or they would not leave even the bones."

"I did not know this," Vance said.

"No reason you should. When I was a child, my grandmother sang to me the songs Logan spoke of tonight. I had not thought of them in years. Of men who defeated dragons, and humans who ruled a world where before they had been hunted for sport. Of ghost-walkers and their tragic end. Of Assassins and kings with bloodlust and a vicious desire to crush their neighbors. I heard my grandmother's voice as Logan addressed the troops. It seemed as though she spoke to me."

"Will you tell me what she said?"

"She whispered that we might emerge victorious. But only if each of us does the impossible."

It seemed to Logan as though Vance had become as frozen as he.

Nicolette went on, "My first challenge, she said, was to forget the past and focus upon the future. Which is why I offer you the hand of friendship."

"I am honored," Vance said.

"And I, for one, am glad to have you at my back," Nicolette replied.

Logan waited until they continued on their rounds. Then he slipped unseen from his corner, padded quietly to his chamber, and slept, and did not dream.

* * *

Logan had never known a full-scale battle. The border skirmishes he had survived had been fierce enough to cost the lives of men, and that was close enough to understand the flavor of combat. He tasted it the next morning and saw it in the eyes of his team. The soldiers were stiff and sullen, the civilians fearing a storm they could not name. He ordered a final training and directed Vance and Nicolette to go hard on any slackers. But they performed well, his crews, and he knew they were as ready as he could make them.

They gathered in the dining hall afterward, the air tense with the knowledge that their waiting was almost over. The hold had no windows. Since liftoff they had lived according to the Outer Rim cycle, as well as it was known. Their dining hall was a comfortable enough place, with space for three times their number. They had turned one section by the kitchen into a sort of ready room. Equipment and unused bedding formed cushions. There was no rank here, and little discipline.

Vance was sprawled on his back in the corner. He lifted his head far enough to eye Logan and ask, "Why can't you shift?"

Sidra, the former rat-faced child, had grown into a sharp-edged woman with spiked hair and a great love of body art. "We don't like that word."

"I meant no offense," Vance said.

"Just the same, you should know better than to use it. The term is offensive."

According to the legends, ghost-walkers who had become turncoats to their own kind and allied themselves to the Assassins had been known as Shifters. Logan had related the old tales to his crew. Added to this were Sidra's nerves. Logan knew tension took her back to the bad old days.

Nicolette saved him from needing to speak. "Our survival depends on trust. The best trust is between friends. Friends give allowances. Even when it costs."

Logan saw Vance nod to his fellow officer. This new harmony between them filled Logan with an uncommon sense of hope. He replied, "To answer your question, I've tried to ghost-walk. Sidra worked with me for months. I never could."

Sidra eased back against the wall. "The legends speak of his kind. The ones who find us. Or did."

"My kind were the first to become Shifters," Logan said. "They were rewarded with palaces and titles. My kind hunted, the Assassins killed."

Nicolette shifted her gaze, and Logan saw the question there in her eyes. He waited for her to ask if his own clan had possessed the talent and become traitors. The answer was, he suspected this but had found no record. But Nicolette returned her gaze to Vance and left the words unspoken. Logan breathed easier.

Vance asked Sidra, "That first time, how did you know what to do?"

She pointed her chin at Logan. "He told me. I was nine and starving. I thought he was a nightwalker come to steal my breath. But he had fed me for months, and he had found me shelter. So I listened. Though he frightened me terribly."

"I had just turned ten," Logan recalled. "Most nights I slept in the scullery where my mother could protect me, for there were predators in the merchant clan. In my heart I knew I was just one step away from where Sidra was."

"Logan did not know what to tell me," Sidra went on. "Only that I should try to move without walking."

"I sensed this ability she didn't even know she had," Logan said. "And then for weeks after, I had a recurring dream. It was exactly what happened."

"I trusted him enough to try, though I thought he was insane." Sidra smiled. "It was the finest day of my life."

Logan saw grins from his team, even the most frightened. They all remembered their first outing.

Vance admitted, "I would like to try that more than anything."

"We have offered," Logan said. "Many times."

"I haven't accepted because the prospect terrifies me." There were nods from many of the soldiers, and Vance asked, "Does it hurt?"

"Not for me," Nicolette replied. "Not yet."

Logan replied, "I've done it a hundred times and more. And I'm still scared. But never is there any discomfort. I take their hand, I step forward with them, and I am there."

One of Vance's team asked, "Can you go anywhere?"

"Anywhere we have been before," Sidra replied.

"And that is the catch," Logan said. "That's why Nicolette and Sidra must perform the first duty when we arrive. It must happen before we make landfall. While they do not know why we've come."

As though in confirmation, the ship's gong sounded. Logan rose and said, "First team, prepare yourselves. Vance, Nicolette, Sidra, come with me."

* * *

As they walked a long iron tunnel, through the crew's quarters and another mess hall, Sidra drew Logan back far enough to hiss, "I can handle this first duty alone."

Logan pointed to where Vance and Nicolette stood before the steel portal leading to the flight deck. "Study them well. Let them teach you by example."

"Did you not hear what I said?"

"And I answered you. Why do you think they're here at all?"

"They are military." Her mouth shaped one word, her face another.

"They understand how to form and lead a team. Your chance to do the same will come soon enough. You must learn everything they have to teach you." Logan walked away. A moment passed, then Sidra followed.

When they joined the pair by the access door, Vance murmured, "You are a better man than you let on."

The door slid open while Logan was still searching for a response. The four of them entered the flight deck and froze.

The flight deck was rimmed by a steel rail forming an interplanetary balcony. Before them was a wall of stars.

A fraction of Logan's brain said he had to be looking at giant monitors. But most of his mind was as immobilized as his body. He stared at the center of the galaxy. Seeing a photograph and staring at the view from space were entirely different. Before him a vast blanket of stars formed a cloud of fire and splendor. The colors were without name, the brilliance almost blinding.

Captain Hattie was a brusque woman with the hands of a bricklayer and a voice to match. "You've never been to space?"

Logan licked his lips, swallowed, then managed, "No, ma'am."

"You may address me as Captain Hattie or Skipper. All right. Enough gawking." She glowered at them. "Listen up. I won't be hauling anybody's ashes home, no matter what some general might think. You buy the farm on Aldwyn, you rot here. Read me?"

"Aye, Skipper."

She said to her pilot, "Swing the image." The sky pivoted to the right. Gradually a dark mass bit a slice from the stars to their right, and their destination came into view.

Aldwyn was a planetary name from the distant past, and in the old tongue the word meant *thief*. Eons ago, the wandering planet was said to steal away men's breath, turning them old before their time. The miners called it the Dead World and took pride in its title. Aldwyn was a tomb of slag and glistening rock, adorned with little save frozen streams of lava.

The scientists had argued for centuries over how Aldwyn came to be. The current theory was that it was in fact an orphan world. At some point in the far-distant past, a sun had gone nova, blasting its core in a furious display that had consumed all the inner worlds. But Aldwyn had been expelled, cast from its orbit and sent to wander the empty reaches. Centuries passed beyond count until the Cygneus star had captured it. Which was a very good thing indeed, despite the ancient fables. For Aldwyn was filled to bursting with treasure.

There was gold to be had and a multitude of other precious metals. But most valuable of all was an element found nowhere else. Ditrinium, the scientists named it. A miner's weight of rarified ditrinium promised a lifetime of wealth and ease. Ditrinium now formed the heart of their most potent weapons and transports. It defined who ruled the Cygnean system.

Gradually Aldwyn had been parceled out between the most powerful clans. All but one small segment, a pirate's haven known as the Outer Rim. It had been ruled by outlaw fiefs for eons. So long, in fact, that some suggested it was time to recognize the Outer Rim as a nation unto itself. But it was controlled by a clan that still preyed on others. They had no interest in joining anyone. They took pleasure from the warrior's creed. The clan's name was Havoc.

Captain Hattie said, "Those lights you see in the bottom right—that's supposedly our destination. You know it?"

"Loghir, capital of Aldwyn," Logan said. "In the old tongue it means 'lost lands.'"

She grunted approval. "The lights mark the mine heads and the landing site. The city's mostly underground." She pointed to the curved border where the stars met the planet. "The Outer Rim is beyond the horizon there to your left. If you want my advice, you'd be better off not splitting your troops."

"Four of my team members have to make landfall at Loghir," Logan insisted.

"Whatever your reasons, they're as insane as your being here at all," Hattie barked.

"We're wasting time," Logan said.

Biting down on her argument gave her voice a savage note. She stomped about and yelled, "Ready the pod!"

12

The Messenger guards who came for Sean and Dillon were polite and very alert. They brought two fresh uniforms, Academy cadet green and Attendant grey-blue. But every emblem had been removed from both, including the buttons. Sean felt slightly queasy as he sealed the seams of his jacket and trousers, thinking the outfits had been specifically made for their trial.

They traveled to the surface by way of a glass-tube elevator rising from the internment levels to a judiciary forecourt. It was the first time Sean had seen the sky in a week. The guards were evidently used to inmates needing a moment to adjust. They hovered but did not push. There was no need for the guards to keep hold, as the clamps attached to their ankles kept the twins in place.

Sean took a slow look around. The sky had never seemed so beautiful. Every cloud was a work of art. The mild wind carried a chilly whisper of farewell. He had not missed his freedom so much as at that very moment. Now it formed a bone-deep ache.

The guard said, "That's it. Let's move."

The forecourt to the Halls of Justice was a stone-walled circle carved from a much larger plaza. The floor was inlaid with the galactic-sunburst emblem of the Human Assembly. All around the plaza, people stopped and stared at their passage.

Dillon muttered, "I don't get it."

Sean nodded but did not speak.

"We've committed the crime of the century?" Dillon glanced over his shoulder. "Everybody's still watching us."

The justice building was shaped like a palace from some Arabian nightmare. Round towers rose from a pale building with softly curved corners. Seven turrets soared high overhead. Seven flagstaffs pierced the sky like spears. The stairs and the doors and the foyer were all oversized and very grand. Sean tried to tell himself it was all meant to intimidate. Repeating that helped—not much, but a little.

They passed through the massive portal, crossed the foyer, and climbed stairs that curved around a huge rotunda. They entered a windowless courtroom that formed another incomplete circle. The Assembly's sunburst was repeated twice, inlaid into the raised wooden dais where the three tribune Justices would sit, and carved into the rear wall. A dozen empty pews formed ranks between them and the dais.

Their escorts pointed the twins forward, then positioned themselves by the rear portal. A third guard entered and took up station by a smaller door beside the Justices' dais. The chamber's only other occupants were their former Advocate Cylian and a man who stood with his back to the room.

The Advocate shot them a look, her blank mask still in place, then went back to her whispered conversation with the man. The pair stood between a small front door and three rows of seats that rose like giant steps by the side wall. Sean assumed the seats were for the Assembly's version of a jury. Or maybe they required a certain number of official witnesses for an execution. He swallowed hard. His lack of knowledge filled the chamber like sulfurous smoke.

As they walked the central aisle, Sean murmured, "It's not too late. We can still ask the Advocate for her help."

Dillon snorted. "All she'll do is help tie the noose."

"I'm serious."

"And I'm telling you it doesn't matter." Dillon's face was so tight it appeared bloodless. "This whole deal is over before it starts."

"Thanks for the vote of confidence."

"I kept expecting somebody to show up and rescue us," Dillon replied. "Think about it. We've got a whole planet in our debt. Not to mention all those people we worked with—Carver, Tatyana, Elenya's father . . ."

"Forget her family. Elenya's mom is probably watching this and cheering."

"Still, none of those people could spare a few minutes to find out what happened to us?"

Sean slipped behind the front table. "I wondered about that too."

"They've obviously been blocked," Dillon said. "We're cut off from our allies."

Sean settled into the padded chair. "But why?"

"Same reason all those people around the plaza stopped and watched us. This thing is a lot bigger than helping Carey's cousin."

Sean studied his brother. "You're not nearly as dumb as you look."

Dillon offered the first smile in what felt like years. "I'm smart enough to know you need to handle this one. Not some flunky assigned by the guy who wants to sink our boat."

The guard by the front portal snapped to attention and called, "All rise."

Kaviti said, "The accused may be seated."

Ambassador Kaviti was the oldest of the three Justices, but only by a few years. The other two were female. One was a handsome, dark-skinned woman who glared at them with Zulu intensity.

Dillon indicated her with a jerk of his chin and murmured, "I know about that one."

"Tell me."

"She used to teach at the Academy. A couple of years ago they ran her off. Too tough."

Sean glanced over. "Is that a joke?"

"Watch closely," Dillon replied. "This is me not laughing."

The third Justice was a rotund white-haired woman who wore her rumpled uniform like a bathrobe with buttons. Any hope of grandmotherly affection, however, was erased by a single glimpse of those merciless grey eyes.

Kaviti occupied the central chair. He addressed the woman standing by the empty jury box. "Assume your position, Advocate. Let us begin."

"Begging the Justices' pardon," Cylian replied. "I have been dismissed."

"Dismissed? By whom?"

"The accused, Your Honor."

"This is outrageous," Kaviti sputtered. "Cadets refusing counsel? I've never heard of such nonsense."

"Nonetheless, Your Honor, it is their right as accused—"

"Rubbish." Kaviti aimed across the distance at Sean. "You there. Sean Kirrel. I am hereby ordering you to accept the wisdom of your betters."

Sean rose to his feet. "Gladly, Your Honor. But only if you permit us to appoint our own Advocate."

Kaviti sniffed. "Out of the question. Advocate Cylian is perfectly suited to the task at hand."

"She is also on your personal staff," Sean replied.

"Tribunal Justices are tasked to remain impartial. Advocate Cylian was appointed to serve your best interests."

"Just the same," Sean replied, "your own assistant has said it's our right to make the selection."

"Unacceptable," Kaviti snapped. "We intend to complete these proceedings without further—"

"Point of order," the Zulu Justice said.

Kaviti sniffed again but subsided.

The dark-skinned woman said, "Kirrel, is it?"

"Yes, Your Honor. Sean Kirrel."

"Explain yourself."

"This entire proceeding is a charade," Sean said. "And Kaviti knows it."

"You will refer to him as 'Ambassador' or 'Your Honor,'" she replied, but without heat. "Do you realize you could face years of incarceration?"

Sean glanced at his brother, which was a very good thing. Dillon's gaze carried the confident rage that had seen them through numerous early battles. His look said all. He had Sean's back and total confidence in his brother's ability.

Kaviti snapped, "Answer the question."

Sean directed his words to the Zulu. "Can I ask a question of my own?"

"Very well."

"Who brought these charges against us? I'll bet it was Kaviti."

"I will not warn you again as to the proper form of address." She fingered her tablet as she spoke.

"Was it him? Because I'm pretty sure the charges don't have anything to do with our actions, and everything to do with him hating me from the first day I set foot—"

"Silence!" Kaviti said.

The Zulu passed her tablet to the dumpy woman. "I for one would like to hear the cadet's full response."

"This is a waste of the court's time," Kaviti muttered.

"Nonetheless." The Zulu motioned to Sean. "Continue."

"You heard him yourself, Your Honor. First he orders us to take his own assistant as our counsel. Then he claims that he's totally impartial. Now you discover that he's the one who—"

"I've heard enough of this garbage!" Kaviti's face was beet red. "The accused will sit down and this court will proceed with its judgment!"

The man who had been standing in the jury box's shadow stepped forward and said, "Point of order, if the court allows."

13

The Outer Rim was dominated by a man named Tiko, who had claimed for himself the title of duke. It was possible that his forebears might once have ruled a fief, but the Outer Rim was a place earned through battle and lies and subterfuge, and it was just as likely that Tiko had invented the title when he bulled his way into the ruler's cavern.

One thing could be said about Tiko without risk. He was a survivor. He had ruled his segment of the Outer Rim for thirty-seven years, longer than anyone in living memory. He had used the time well, building defenses that had brought down the invading fleet. Up until that victory, Tiko had allowed the smaller fiefs to maintain their mines and their townships, so long as they bent the knee to his rule and paid their dues to his coffers. But once he had defeated the Cygnean battalion, he became hungry for more power and more mines. Slowly, steadily, he began devouring the smaller clans.

To those mini fiefs rich enough to afford strong defenses

of their own, he took a different approach. The Outer Rim reservoirs were all within Tiko's territory. So he slowly began cutting off their supplies.

All this Logan knew from reports sent back by the governing council's representatives on Loghir. There was supposed to be a strict quarantine against the Outer Rim, but their mines were rich, and Cygneus was a long way off. The Loghir black market kept the outer fiefs from dying of thirst. Even so, for many of the smaller Outer Rim fiefdoms, water was more valuable than a man's life.

Which was why Logan had chosen his cargo.

For Logan's plan to work, he needed what Nicolette called an outlier station. Logan felt the name did not apply to what they intended. But he didn't object, mostly because plans like theirs had never been attempted before.

The transport pods were shaped like giant metal seeds. Captain Hattie had a perfectly good reason for sending a pod to the planet's capital. The skies above Aldwyn were thick with ships, and those that carried time-sensitive cargos bribed their way into a quick berth. Such negotiations were best carried out in person, so Hattie radioed a request to the city's terminal and the transport was granted passage.

Once the pod left with Nicolette and her three teammates, Hattie made no more outright criticisms of their plans. But her grumbling filled the flight deck, and her crew ducked every time her gaze shifted. Logan made no attempt to hide himself away, and Vance remained firmly by his side.

Finally the captain snarled, "What now?"

"I must communicate with someone in the Outer Rim," Logan said.

She glared across the steel deck. "Explain yourself."

"Here's what I know," Logan continued. "The Outer Rim has a main landing site. And then there is a smaller one tucked well away. This second site is in disputed territory. A number of outlaw fiefs claim the surrounding region. The landing strip is used by all and is the one point where they do not battle. Anyone who breaks the peace is banned."

She squinted at him. "You know this how?"

He met her gaze. "The question is, do you know this second site?"

"I do."

"Ping the site's control tower," Logan said. "Tell them I have a delivery for Linux Hawk."

***

"What manner of pup dares order me about?"

The face glaring from Captain Hattie's monitor was aged but still very handsome, almost refined. Linux wore his white hair with dignity, carefully tended and swept back from a high forehead. His face was seamed, his eyes as dark as the planet he called home. Logan thought he looked like a soft-spoken killer with a taste for the good life.

"I salute you, Uncle," Logan said.

Linux did not respond as Logan had expected, with suspicion and questions only a clansman could answer. Instead, he squinted and leaned closer to the screen. "You're the Count's whelp."

"Aye, sir. I am."

"You carry the look of him. Are you a fighter as well?"

Vance spoke from behind his right shoulder. "That he is, sir."

The old man's gaze did not waver. "How did you know to find me?"

"As a child I heard you had carved out a haven for those who survived and were ready to give up marauding."

"Give up dying, you mean. It was true enough, once. But you've come at a bad time."

"I know that."

"You know, and yet you came?" He snorted. "You show as much sense as your old man."

"I do not seek refuge, I've come to offer it," Logan replied. "What's more, I bring water."

The old man could not quite hide his avaricious gleam. "How much?"

"A million dekaliters," Logan replied. "The ship carries nothing else."

"Then you are welcome," his uncle declared. "I will arrange—"

Logan broke in with, "First there is the small matter of what I want in return."

＊

Nicolette and her team traveled back by holding Sidra's hand. They stood in the rear hold of their vessel a thousand leagues above the point where they had been an instant before. Once she reported in, Logan returned to the flight deck with Vance and said it was time to land. Hattie asked if he was abandoning the team he had sent to Loghir, for the only word she had received from her pod crew was a radio message that Logan's team had entered the city and not returned. Logan did not respond.

Hattie let Logan and Vance remain on the flight deck for the final approach. Logan suspected she hoped it would frighten them from taking what she saw as a suicidal next step. But Logan had found great strength in Sidra's report, not to mention Linux's agreeing to his terms. He watched the planet's approach with awe and more than a little fear. But mostly he was excited by the prospect of what awaited him. Years of hoping. A lifetime spent searching out this one chance, no matter how slender. Logan was far less worried than most would be in this situation, for he had survived many lean and dangerous days. He watched in utter astonishment as the Outer Rim came into view, his worries all centered on those who had put their trust in his untested abilities.

The planet's outer half remained in perpetual darkness. During the period soon after its former sun went nova, a massive object had struck its molten surface. Scientists assumed the impact was what had sent Aldwyn reeling out of its orbit and eventually into its new planetary home. The impact zone was large enough to swallow Logan's entire home province. The crater was rimmed by razor mountains, tall as death's own crown. In eons past, the crater had become home to pirate fiefs, clans who had lost their lands through war. The desperado attitude lived on.

The signal officer reported nervously, "We have been pinged, Skipper. Twice."

"Hold to the course." Hattie sounded calm, but Logan could see her white-knuckle grip on the chair arms. "Identify the source."

"First ping was the main landing terminal. Second ping is our destination, the tower of the lesser field. Now a third ping, Captain! And a fourth! Both originating from planetary weapons systems!"

"Hold fast to your course," she told her frightened pilot.

"The main tower is demanding to know who we are." The signal officer's voice lifted a full octave. "They are threatening to shoot us down if we don't respond!"

"Hold to strict silence!"

"A fifth ping, Captain!"

Logan turned and nodded. Hattie barked, "Send the response. Do it!"

The signal officer slapped the panel hard. Linux had supplied them with both an approach vector and a response signal. The signal was to be their only communication, sent after the fifth ping. Hattie had received the instructions herself and watched as the signal officer coded in the electronic response. Even so, the entire flight deck held their breath in unison until the officer breathed, "All silent, Captain. The weapons systems have unlocked."

"Ready the ship for landing," Hattie said. She turned to Logan and said, "You'd best go prepare your crew for their final approach."

14

The court most certainly does *not* allow," Kaviti snapped.

"Point of order, Honored Justice." The man stepped away from the jury box. "The court has no choice. It is within my right."

The Advocate rose from her position on the front pew. "Ambassador, perhaps it missed your attention, but Commander Taunton has formally registered his interest in the proceedings."

Kaviti demanded, "Why am I just hearing about this now?"

"I was only informed upon arrival in the court." Advocate Cylian seated herself, then glanced at Sean. For the briefest instant, so swift it would have been possible to believe it had not happened at all, the Kabuki mask dissolved and she smiled.

Kaviti missed it because he was scowling at the newcomer. "Formal notice of interest permits you observer status, nothing more."

"True, unless the accused elect to change my status," the newcomer replied. "I formally request the court's permission to address the young men before you."

"Oh, let him," the fake grandmother said. "He's going to in the end."

And then it happened again. While Kaviti scowled at the stranger, the woman shot Sean a look as swift as the Advocate's. And offered him the day's second ray of hope.

The man bowed. "I am most grateful for the court's indulgence."

Dillon jerked to his feet and hissed, "Stand up." When Sean rose, Dillon whispered, "Say yes."

"To what?"

"To anything he says."

Taunton was a small man, half a head shorter than Sean. But he carried himself with such authority that the physical elements were meaningless. He asked Dillon, "You know who I am?"

"Yes, Commander."

"That makes things easier. Introduce your brother, please."

"Commander Taunton, this is Sean Kirrel."

"A pleasure, I'm sure. Are you two willing to appoint me as your Advocate?"

"Out of the question," Kaviti said.

"Yes, Commander," Sean replied.

Taunton then offered Sean the day's third gift. Not a smile so much as the expression of a hungry tiger. All teeth and rage. He leaned forward and murmured, "Then let the games begin."

"If it pleases the court," Taunton said, "might I inquire as to when the prosecutor will arrive?"

It seemed to Sean that Kaviti's ire carried a new and nervous tone. "This is a preliminary hearing. A prosecutor is not required to be present."

"And yet the Advocate assigned to the young men by your own office told them that charges were already leveled. Quite serious charges. Is that not so?"

"If she did so, it was without my knowing."

Sean looked over to where the Advocate sat behind the empty left-hand table. Her mask was firmly back in place. But she must have felt his eyes, for she shot him a glance and gave a fractional head shake. Sean turned back around.

"Even so." Taunton stood before their table, hands laced behind his back. "Does it not appear a bit strange that a *prosecutor* would level such *extremely severe* charges and not feel required to attend the first hearing?"

Kaviti appeared to be the only Justice willing to speak. "Certainly not."

"I thank the court for this most illuminating clarification."

"If that is all, the court hereby orders the Kirrel brothers to be returned to their—"

"One moment, if it pleases the court." Taunton made a process of drawing papers from his pocket and unfolding them. "It appears that the prosecutor's name has been omitted from the court documents."

"Justices are entitled to bring charges," Kaviti replied. "Which you would know, if you had any foundation—"

"And yet do these same rules of procedure not require the Justice to then *immediately* appoint a prosecutor? Following this, are they not required to *immediately* excuse themselves from all court proceedings?"

The Zulu said, "That is correct."

Kaviti snarled, "I have already stated that this is a preliminary hearing only, and thus none of these rules apply, as you would know if you had any business—"

"Ah, but it *is* my business, honored sir. These young men have made it my business. Have you not, Sean? Dillon?"

"Definitely, yes."

"Absolutely."

"Let it be so noted." Taunton returned his attention to the Justices. "Now that this matter has been resolved, allow me to raise another. Am I correct in assuming you have imprisoned these young men on charges that were not formally registered?"

Kaviti bridled. "How dare you enter this court uninvited and imply—"

"And they have been incarcerated for six days—can that truly be so?"

Kaviti snarled, "They resisted arrest."

Taunton seemed to take exquisite pleasure in drawing forth another document. "Ah, but I have taken the liberty of gathering testimony of numerous witnesses who claim the exact opposite."

The grandmotherly Justice looked askance at the central Justice. "Is this true? You involved me on a false premise?"

Kaviti rose to his feet and thundered, "How *dare* you!"

"How *dare* I?" Taunton grew in size and volume until he filled the space between their table and the dais. "How dare *I*? *You* are seeking to serve as investigator, prosecutor, judge, and jury. How dare *I*? You order them to take as Advocate a member of your personal staff, and *you* ask this of *me*?"

"You will be silent!"

"Let the records show that I hereby accuse *you*, Ambassador Kaviti, of breach of judiciary trust and illegal use of your court-appointed position! Furthermore, I accuse you of reckless abandonment of every principle that underpins the Human Assembly!"

"Those two boys—"

"These two *men*, my clients, did nothing whatsoever except respond to an emergency appeal. They saved an innocent civilian from being dismembered, and a high political official of their home world from being coerced into making a terrible choice—go against his principles or condemn his nephew to a slow and painful death."

"Now, see here—"

Taunton stabbed the air over their table. "These two are *heroes*. They have precisely obeyed the Human Assembly's covenant. They have always acted as servants to our code of ethics and behavior! How dare *I*? This is how I respond, sir. I will go before the Assembly and request—no, *demand*— that you be stripped of all titles and positions. *That* is what I dare." He turned his back on the Justices and said, "Come, lads. We are done with this travesty."

Kaviti sputtered, "I have not dismissed them!"

"Might I suggest," the Zulu murmured, "that now would be a good time to remain silent."

Taunton led them back to where the guards stood at rigid attention. He pointed to Dillon's ankle clamp and ordered, "Free these men."

15

ogan returned to his team as the ship descended into an underground hold. And there they waited. His uncle Linux insisted upon testing the water's purity before letting anyone disembark. This cost Logan's team two precious hours. But he did not complain because it would have accomplished nothing.

Finally the claxon sounded. When the deck portal rumbled down, Logan was astonished to find just one old man. He walked down the steel deck and said, "Greetings, Uncle."

The man was tall and carried a severe strength that defied his silver-white mane. "I would say that it is an honor, but to begin with lies is unworthy of us both."

Logan searched the massive cavern. It was entirely empty save for their ship, Linux, and an open-topped ground transport. "You come alone?"

"I saw no need to risk the lives of others." Linux gestured to the transport. "Load your team. How many are you?"

"Fifty-two."

"Not enough." He watched them troop down the rear deck. "Where are their weapons?"

"In their packs."

"You carry no artillery?"

"The last invasion tried that and failed," Logan replied. "I have a different plan in mind."

Black eyes glittered with a humor Logan could only call evil. "When you meet your father, be sure and give him my best."

***

Linux had a slow way of talking that made a man feel comfortable, though his news was dire. "My fief controls the largest of the perimeter markets. Or rather, we once ran things. Now the Havoc dogs are gnawing on our borders, and many of the merchants have been scared off."

"They want to starve you out," Vance said.

"They want us to die," Linux said. He drove the transport with grim intent. "Tell me, Lord Hawk, how is it you journey with these folk, the enemy of your people?"

"They are friends, I find them trustworthy, and they shield my back," Logan replied. "Who could ask for more?"

"You of all people should know the Cygnean methods. The Aldus clan slaughtered your kin."

"They defeated us," Logan agreed. "But even my father says they won a fair fight."

"There is no such thing," Linux countered. "Except in history books written by the victors."

"A fair battle, fairly won," Logan said. "I have studied their tactics, and they deserved to win."

Linux chewed on that for a time. "So you joined them."

"So I could come here."

"And die with your starving kin, at the boundary of a market Clan Havoc will soon claim as their own."

Linux's transport was a metal beast that easily held Logan's entire team and all their gear. The driver's roofless cab had twin seats up front with a padded row behind. Logan sat beside Linux. Vance and Nicolette shared the rear seat with Sidra. The market cave was so vast the far side was lost to smoke and dust.

Linux smiled at their astonishment. "At its height, Hawk's Market had almost two thousand stallholders. We were always fair in our dealings. We kept order. We stayed honest. Before the troubles started, we were turning merchants away."

Vance asked, "And now?"

"We've lost several hundred thus far. Still more depart every day."

Even so, the market was jammed and noisy. The merchants and customers made way reluctantly for the transport. Linux held to the central thoroughfare, broad as a Cygnean highway, and moved at scarcely more than a walking pace. For once, Logan felt no impatience. He studied the place and the people, hunting.

Linux went on, "Every time Clan Havoc sends in their packs of dogs, more of the easily frightened depart. The others watch and hope that we will find a solution. Our situation is dire enough for me to hope you might succeed, when I know it is impossible."

Logan said, "I thank you for this gift of trust."

Linux shook his head. "Understand me, nephew. I do not trust any Cygnean soldier. But I am trapped, and the Havoc dogs will soon be baying for my hide."

This cavern held not just a market but a township. The stalls backed up against stone houses, most with upper floors sprouting balconies that overlooked the fray. There were factories and inns and music and even songbirds in gilded cages. The smells were strong, the din more powerful still. Linux pointed down various sidelines, listing the occupants. In the far distance rose glass-roofed structures housing the hydroponics gardens.

At several points Logan spotted the crest of Hawk's Fief—adorning the sides of buildings, painted on signposts, and the largest emblem of all carved above passages leading from the cavern. Logan studied his clan's ancient battle standard, the attacking bird of prey at its heart, and felt something stir in his gut. What precisely, he could not say, only that his father felt unexpectedly close.

The market's distant ceiling was a true marvel. A center portion, perhaps two hundred paces across, was a circle of glass. The stars swam and flowed overhead as the transport moved along, for the aperture was far from perfectly formed.

"There are any number of such caverns," Linux said, following Logan's astonished gaze. "At least a dozen in the Outer Rim alone. Star domes, they're called. What you see there is thicker than the height of five men. The material is carbonized and harder than most stone."

A fitting home for Hawk's Fief, Logan wanted to say, but he was silenced by the market's sudden change.

As they approached the cavern's side, the market became quieter. The people they passed wore sullen gazes and scowled when they recognized Linux.

Here the market reminded Logan of an old man's mouth, with empty spaces where stone teeth should have resided. They passed several where the stall and the house behind had been reduced to rubble.

Linux remained silent as he drove them toward the cavern's wall. He stopped where the avenue entered a massive tunnel. "Eighteen leagues dead ahead, you enter the Havoc fief. When we began here, the distance separating our two clans was more than enough. They had their world, we had ours."

Nicolette said, "You could block it off."

Linux responded by turning right and heading down a side lane. "We survive by taking no offense. We pretend all is well. We offer fealty. We hope Tiko will forget these wild ambitions and return to peace."

Logan surveyed a cluster of seven structures, all bearing the Hawk's crest, all empty. "How is that working for you?"

Linux halted before the largest of the structures. "This was home to our militia. We shifted them to the market's far end to reduce the risk of conflict. You are welcome to it."

Logan did not move. "Tell me the rest."

Linux kneaded the wheel with two strong hands. He did not speak.

Logan guessed, "There are some in your company who want to attack before you grow weaker still."

"Their numbers grow with every passing day."

"They should have a talk with my father," Logan said. "See how far that strategy took him."

Linux cast him a look of dark approval. "It is claimed Clan Havoc now holds the technology required to make ditrinium weaponry."

"Which was how they defeated our forces," Nicolette said. "We suspected as much, but there were no survivors to confirm it."

Logan asked, "You have ditrinium?"

"The mine and the smelting operations. The finest in the Outer Rim."

"This conflict was never about the market," Vance said. "The Havoc fief wants your mine."

"Duke Tiko wants everything," Linux replied.

Logan saw the pieces fit together. "He wants to rule Aldwyn."

"If he manages to take over all of the Outer Rim and lay claim to the planet," Vance said, "all he'd need to do is threaten to cut off the supply of ditrinium. The ruling council on Cygneus would snap like a dry twig."

"Which would put the entire system within Tiko's reach," Nicolette said.

Logan said, "General Brodwyn didn't allow us to come because of the Assembly."

Nicolette looked confused. "But she's certain we will fail."

"The general doesn't care what happens to us," Vance said,

his humor gone now. "If we confirm Tiko's plans, we have succeeded. Whether we live or die is unimportant."

Linux did not actually smile, but humor tightened the seams around his eyes. "And I thought my own situation was dire."

16

Commander Taunton led Sean and Dillon back across the circular forecourt and into the main plaza. They were followed by the silent Advocate. Taunton noticed the direction of Sean's scowl and said, "Cylian risked her position to alert me."

Sean stifled his protest. But he wasn't satisfied. Not by a long shot. Dillon apparently agreed, for he muttered, "She could have warned us. Should have, in fact."

Taunton replied, "I specifically directed her to keep you in the dark. If Kaviti had even suspected what I planned, he would have found a way to block my entry."

Dillon did not respond.

Taunton indicated the people who watched their progress across the plaza. "As it is, I was able to alert allies within the Assembly. As did your assigned Advocate. Too many people know about this travesty of justice now. Kaviti can't pretend it didn't take place."

Dillon asked, "What will happen to him?"

"Forced retirement, I hope. At the very least, I'm expecting a public rebuke."

Sean exchanged a glance with his brother. Dillon was equally unimpressed. "So, you'd be happy with a slap on the wrist?"

"Actually, I would. Quite satisfied, in fact."

Dillon protested, "That joker locked us up. He did his best to strip away our futures."

Taunton pointed them between two buildings that looked like Grecian temples on steroids. The paving stones and the sides to all the buildings were etched and colored with the planetary emblems of a hundred and nineteen worlds. "You're free," he replied. "You are both reinstated. In fact, in the eyes of many your status has been elevated."

Cylian spoke for the first time since addressing the tribunal. "Not to mention how Kaviti's faction has been handed a public censure."

"Precisely." Taunton's goal was a stone bench overlooking the chest-high wall rimming the cliff. Dillon had never been here before, so he did what every first visitor did, which was gape. Beyond the wall was a six-hundred-foot drop, down to a ribbon of beach the same color as the stone plaza. The largest ocean on Serena stretched out before them.

Dillon whistled at the drop. "What's to keep people from taking a dive?"

"There's a shield rimming the whole plaza," Sean said.

"For real?"

"It's too far out to touch, but if you toss a stone it will spark."

Dillon caught Sean's expression and said, "Elenya brought you here?"

There was no need to tell them how he and Elenya had selected a bench farther along the rim as their very own.

He waited until Dillon had taken a seat beside the commander. Then he said, "What did you mean by Kaviti's faction?"

Taunton jerked his chin at Cylian. "Tell them."

She settled against the wall beside Sean and said, "Within the Assembly there is a secretive group seeking power. Kaviti is one of their more outspoken members."

Taunton told Dillon, "There's a great deal more at stake than the arrest of you and your brother."

Sean realized Dillon was the focal point. Sean felt jarred and bruised by the day's events, not to mention the jail time. He preferred to have this chance to step back and observe. Taunton's words confirmed his suspicions that the commander had not involved himself in order to correct an injustice. The false imprisonment of two brothers was not something that would attract this man's attention. Taunton wanted something.

Taunton continued, "I represent a faction that is troubled by how some within the Assembly believe they are above the law. Thanks to Cylian, we have transformed your shadow trial into a public display of their abuses. We are in the process of preparing for a very real and very serious—"

"I accept," Dillon said.

Taunton leaned back.

"You brought me here to sell me on the idea of helping. Fine. Save your windup. I'm ready."

Taunton exchanged a glance with Cylian. "Actually, it was the Advocate who alerted me to your potential."

"Your files are most impressive," she said.

"Right now, I need an individual with your character, combined with a warrior's training," Taunton went on. He looked at Sean. "I am certain there will be a role for you as well."

Sean shook his head. "I'm not really interested in enlisting."

Cylian frowned in disappointment, but Taunton said, "Your sentiments are understandable, given what you've just been through. Perhaps in time you will reconsider."

Sean doubted it. "Maybe."

"I will count that as an affirmative." Taunton pointed out over the cliff. "Be so good as to tell me what is missing from this scene."

Dillon frowned at the request. But Sean knew what the commander meant. "No storms, no tides, no waves, no currents," he said. "Serena has no moons."

"Correct." Taunton waved at the endless sheet of blue. "Visitors see this and think, 'How peaceful. How calm. How safe.' But down below the surface, monsters roam."

Dillon said, "I thought the Serenese monster was a myth."

"That is as intended. Centuries ago, the sea beasts were expunged from public records. It was a futile and silly act. History has been rewritten by people who prefer good publicity to the truth. The monsters were considered a threat to their concept of idyllic superiority."

Cylian said, "Serena has not known war in two thousand years. They claim to live in peace with all things. The Serenese people like to assume that they discovered the ancient records because Serena is the center of the human universe."

Taunton snorted his disdain. "Back in the age of seagoing vessels, the monsters preyed upon isolated ships. Convoys were never touched, so it was easy to ignore the few survivors who spoke of beasts so large they consumed entire vessels in one gulp." He pointed out beyond the stone wall. "These supposedly calm waters are a fitting metaphor for today's Assembly. On the surface, all is orderly and tranquil. But down below, hidden by shadows and legal design, monsters prey on the weak and gather strength."

"Kaviti," Sean said.

"He is most certainly one of them, but less powerful than he wishes. Others see him as a threat to their secret ways. He is pompous, and he reckons he should be supreme leader. He was easy prey. The ones we suspect are in control may use this as a means of disposing of him."

Sean asked, "Why are we here?"

"I and a few concerned others are bound together in a struggle to uphold the Human Assembly's founding principles." Taunton's gaze never left Dillon. "It is not too late for you to retreat. The task I have in mind could cost you everything. Hunting such a secretive enemy is not without dire peril."

Dillon replied, "It feels like I've spent my whole life waiting for somebody to speak those words."

Taunton nodded. "Go back to the Academy and pack your bags. You will only be returning there to teach."

17

Logan opted to bivouac his crew in the empty militia headquarters. The structure was far too big. The public rooms were intended for squads five times their own size. But if they were successful, the space would come in handy. Plus there was only one main access point, broad double doors at the top of three wide stairs. A second portal was intended for deliveries and protected by the same steel shutters that were locked down over the two front windows. At the rear of the building, a trio of hydroponics sheds flanked the cavern wall. The gardens were full of ripening fruit and vegetables.

They set up camp, prepared a meal, and gorged themselves with the deliberate intent of people who did not know if they would ever eat again.

Logan then set the first teams in place. Their practice sessions had been based around ten teams of four, five on and five off, plus spotters that Logan now set on the headquarters roof, by the Havoc tunnel mouth, and farther along the main thoroughfare. He had intended to use Vance as leader of one shift and Nicolette for the other, but they'd asked to take part in the first series of random strikes together.

Every team was to operate within sight of another, linked all the way back to their headquarters. When they moved anywhere, they would maintain visual contact with the next unit. As he checked their comm links, Logan repeated the words he hoped were imprinted into all their brains. "Our first aim is not to capture every single enemy. We strike, we disappear, we remain safe. And the primary goals of these first sweeps are . . . what?"

Nicolette and Vance responded for their crews. "Sow uncertainty and fear."

"Hold for my signal."

Logan now wore three communication rings. One was connected to his teams on an open link. There was no specialized link for his officers—everyone heard it all. They were frontline troops operating in tandem. Logan intended to reward trust with trust. Another comm ring connected to the ship, the third to Linux. All three worked through the same earpiece, which meant his crew could hear Logan code in the ship and ask to speak with Hattie.

When the skipper came online, Logan asked, "Is this a secure link?"

"You think I'd use anything else?"

"I have a message for General Brodwyn."

"Speak."

"Everything she fears about Clan Havoc is true," Logan said. "And more besides."

"Noted." There was an instant's hesitation, then Hattie added, "Good hunting."

He coded in the link for Linux, and when the old man answered, Logan asked, "All your men are pulled back?"

"As you requested."

"The merchants' private guards know to remain inside?"

"They have been warned."

The link connecting Logan to his team glowed. "Stay ready for my alert. I have to go."

Vance waited for the line to clear, then reported, "We have identified two Havoc teams working the market."

"You're sure they're Havoc?"

"No question." Vance's voice held the languid air of a man who relished danger like another might a fine meal. "I've watched them shake down a merchant with my own eyes."

Nicolette reported in. "A military transport has just emerged from the Havoc tunnel."

Logan felt a slimy claw grip his gut. "Give me the details."

"I count fourteen militia armed to the teeth, plus driver and officer up front. Okay, a second transport has now appeared."

Logan took a long breath. It all came down to this moment. And already his plans were in tatters. "Vance, you are to hold."

"But they're—"

"Do not move. Nicolette, wait for my arrival."

Logan could not be everywhere at once, but he could try. He had kept Sidra in reserve, and when he turned to her now he saw the grin of a feral cat.

She asked, "Where to?"

"This time," Logan replied, "we run."

When Logan arrived at the spotter's position on the thoroughfare, he found the beginning of one nightmare he had not anticipated.

Nicolette gestured as the third transport trundled past below them. "They're coming in force."

"They've changed tactics," Logan realized.

Three transports jammed with armed militia did not make a full-scale invasion. But it was a declaration of intent. Logan fought down a surge of panic as a third transport emerged. The second troop carrier held eighteen plus the driver and officer up front, the third twenty.

Logan coded in his link. "Vance."

"Here."

"Bring your entire team back to the forward position."

"But what about the enemy we've identified — "

"Every second counts. Come now."

"On our way."

They were positioned on a flat roof fronting the main avenue. A waist-high wall ran around the rim. Behind them were an open-air kitchen, two long tables with benches, and several sleeping pallets. Nicolette was prone on Logan's left, her head up just high enough to see over the stone lip. "They must have been planning this for a long time."

Logan turned to Sidra. "Alert all the off-duty teams. Bring them here as fast as you can."

"On it." She vanished.

Logan's senses were on ultra-high alert and his heart raced, yet he maintained a steady intensity. He noted the relaxed savagery in the Havoc militia's expressions. They did not expect any opposition. Why should they? Every incursion they had made thus far had been met by silence and retreat. The duke was upping the stakes, pushing Linux harder. Pressing the advantage. The intended message was clear enough. *Surrender and survive.*

Logan said, "We take the last truck first. Nicolette, your team takes out the driver and officer. Freeze only. Then all the other teams seize hold of the troops."

She squinted. "We don't remove them?"

"No time." Not for binding them or for explanations. "On my mark." He waited for her to give the orders, then said, "Go."

At the scrape of footsteps, Logan glanced around and saw Vance and his team fill the space behind. He motioned his second officer forward, then turned back in time to see Nicolette's top two ghost-walkers reach out and pin the driver and officer where they sat.

The transports were not moving swiftly. Logan assumed their speed was part of the overall strategy. They traveled at hardly more than a walking pace, allowing fear and panic to spread before them. The third truck ambled on for a bit, then veered slightly and finally nudged into the next stall on the avenue's right side. The officer in the middle truck was alerted to something wrong when the stall's central pillar gave with a loud *crack*, and the front awning draped itself over the truck like a dusty blanket.

The second transport halted. The first continued on a bit, then stopped as well. The two officers stood in their respective seats and turned around. They stared back to where the third truck remained trapped halfway inside the stall. There was no motion from it. The second truck's officer shouted something. The militia began readying to disembark.

"Vance—" Logan stopped in mid-command because Vance was already positioning his teams.

A few heartbeats later, activity around the second vehicle was immobilized. The militia froze as they descended from the rear hold, the driver was fixed in mid-turn, and the officer surveyed everything without protest or motion. Now it was only the first truck's officer who shouted.

Sidra reappeared beside Logan. "Three teams are here. The fourth was asleep. They're coming."

Logan pointed to the militia now spreading out from the first transport, approaching their silent team. "Nicolette, have half your team freeze the troops on foot. When that's done, send the others down. Start binding them—ankles and wrists."

When she departed, Logan waved Vance forward. "Have your team take out the first transport."

Nicolette slipped back into position beside Logan. "Smooth as silk."

Together they watched as the troops on patrol halted in their tracks, and the first transport became as motionless as the others.

Logan said, "When the soldiers are bound, all crews should start shifting them to the holding pens inside the militia headquarters. After that, we go hunting."

18

Their new headquarters served as a staging area. The captured Havoc personnel were bound ankle and wrist and mouth, except for three who breathed with difficulty. The trio was warned if they made any sound they would be punished. But the surprise assault left the entire company very subdued.

The headquarters' three large central chambers became jammed with fifty prone bodies. Logan's teams shaped them into blocks of ten, with little avenues separating them. Everyone who was not out hunting helped. Groups of ten prisoners had their hands and feet and mouths released. They were taken on breaks, then sent back to the floor. Logan shifted those on guard duty every hour or so.

And still more prisoners kept arriving.

They worked through the day shift, then the night, and another day. Aldwyn held to a standard Cygnean day. Since there was neither day nor season, the shift of hours hardly mattered.

Logan and his teams were both exhausted and too exhilarated to stop. Spotting the Havoc crews proved easier than expected, as they had been chosen with an intention to intimidate. They were big and they swaggered. They moved in twos and threes, dressed in dark shirts with the Havoc knife-slash on their shoulders. People shied away from them, creating tight circles even in the most crowded lanes.

Vance had an idea, swiftly adopted by Nicolette's teams. When a Havoc crew was identified, the teams' first task was to locate a private space. A Havoc pair or trio was gripped from the waist up, and air was cut off, which rendered them powerless to struggle. They were walked down the lane or into the empty stall. There they were bound and then shipped back to join their fellows in the holding pen.

Logan jumped back and forth. Wherever the action was fierce, Sidra took him. He said very little to the frontline teams because he did not need to. The squads performed beautifully. He complimented Vance and Nicolette as they continued to sweep up the Havoc forces, and did so on the open comm link.

His teams started showing a new air of confidence. The radio chatter became terse, quick fragments shared by people who trusted one another. *Go there. Three in the alley. One caught. Who's on two and three?*

The groups operated in smooth tandem. It was like watching a ballet, only one where the dancers made up the steps as they moved.

Logan wanted to live every moment. See it all. Devour the experience. Because here in the market of a forbidden realm, the hopes he had carried for a lifetime took on physical form.

Gradually word spread among the merchants and the customers and the remaining Havoc militia. A change had come. Something was happening.

Nicolette reported in, "A Havoc crew is holed up in a restaurant. They've sent everyone out. Cooks, staff—they're milling about in the lane."

Vance said, "They know."

More likely, Logan thought, they merely suspected. "I'm on my way."

The restaurant was structured like a street-front café, only here there was no sky to enjoy. The pedestrian traffic had been rendered chaotic by the shop owner and all his staff milling about. Two avenues intersected directly in front of the awning. Chairs littered the eating area, several tables were overturned, and all the customers added their own clamor to the mix.

Logan walked out of the alley where Sidra had brought him. The shops to either side had expanded their trays of merchandise until they blocked his ability to see what was going on. So he stepped over to where Nicolette stood surveying the restaurant.

She greeted him with, "I've seen three different faces come and go before the window and the door. The owner there says six of them entered and ordered everyone to leave."

Vance had arrived by then, and he moved to Logan's other side. "They've probably split their forces, in case we try the rear approach."

"We don't have any choice," Nicolette said. "Going in the front way blows our cover in front of a hundred witnesses. More."

Logan agreed with both of his officers and was about to give the order for a rear assault, when the Havoc crew proved them all wrong.

Only later did he realize they had been waiting for Logan's crew to approach. The four of them—the three officers plus Sidra—were completely different from everyone else. They did not mill about. They did not look distressed. They stood calmly and surveyed the scene with a hunter's eye for the terrain. And the Havoc crew was ready.

The three attackers piled out together, slamming through the restaurant door and spreading out and lifting their guns, so fast that Logan was caught completely by surprise. They held old-fashioned projectile weapons intended to frighten with noise. They fired and moved and fired, emptying their weapons in a matter of seconds. All of them taking aim at Logan, Vance, and Nicolette.

Logan found himself surrounded by a sheet of shimmering air. He watched the shields around Nicolette and Vance vibrate with each bullet, like water struck by stones. Further out, people screamed and fled. By the restaurant, the three stood stock-still, their faces turning red, then blue.

Logan yelled, "Let them breathe!"

Nicolette called, "Teams two and three, take out the remaining three."

As her forces moved in, Logan turned to where Sidra stood. "You shielded me."

"All the time," she replied, and pointed to his officers. "I wasn't sure I could hold four inside my shield. Now I know."

Logan said, "I owe you."

"We all do," Vance said.

Sidra blushed. "We are drawing a crowd."

Logan nodded. "It's time to go."

19

The remaining Havoc crews vanished. The market returned to its frenetic din. If anything, the activity became more frenzied. Logan made several more sweeps with his teams, each revealing the same situation. Merchants and customers alike showed a sense of wonder and disbelief. He saw smiles, even heard laughter.

The comm link supplied by Linux glowed. When Logan answered, his uncle demanded, "Are the reports I hear true?"

"Our initial forays have been successful." Logan leaned against the nearest wall. Even the sense of partial victory was enough to unleash a wave of exhaustion. "We're not in the clear yet. Havoc is bound to retaliate."

"Of that I am absolutely certain." Linux hesitated, then added, "It appears I may have underestimated you."

When Linux cut off, Logan asked Sidra, "Are you as tired as I am?"

"Not until you asked."

They returned to the militia headquarters, where two-thirds of the teams were sacked out. Logan ate a hurried meal standing by the cooks, then asked Nicolette, "When is Loghir's next sleep cycle?"

She checked her readout. "Just under six hours."

"And battalion HQ?"

A slightly longer pause, then she answered, "Day officially begins in five hours."

That did not leave Logan time enough for a proper rest, but it would have to do. He started toward an empty pallet and groaned his way down. "I have to report in. Wake me in four hours."

***

They left four scouting teams in the market, supervised by Nicolette. No ghost-walkers, just the military crew, with orders to stay well down. No heroics, no attempts to halt any Havoc team if they moved. Just keep an eye out. Report any change. Nothing more.

Everyone else started moving prisoners.

The plan was probably flawed in some way or another. Logan was too weary to make any improvements. He woke feeling more exhausted than when he lay down. The same fatigue was imprinted on many other faces.

They did what Vance called "work by numbers." Two prisoners had their wrists freed, and then one arm was bound to the other's, right to left. Their outside arms were strapped tight to their sides. The ghost-walker then moved into place between them, gripped the bound arms, and stepped forward.

Their destination was chosen for maximum impact. Once the prisoner transport was completed, Logan coded in the link to Linux. When the old man answered, Logan said, "I need you to make a call. Do you have a trusted contact in Loghir?"

"Of course."

"Have him contact the head of their police. There is a hotel directly across the square from their headquarters."

"I have stayed there."

"We took five rooms on the top floor. They are now filled with Havoc's forces."

20

Sean went straight to Serena's main hospital. Insgar, the founder of the Watchers' Academy and his primary ally among the highest ranks, had been ill for almost a year. Sandrine, the doctor whom he and Dillon had met at the Cyrian train station, greeted him with the same somber news he had been hearing for months. Insgar slept. She was comfortable. Sandrine would alert him if she rose to full consciousness. Which had not happened since his last visit.

Sean sat by her bedside for a time, missing her scolding voice and guidance more than he knew how to say. Now more than ever, he needed a wise friend.

The next day Sean returned to the loft apartment near Raleigh's main university. He arrived at well after midnight Eastern time. He and Dillon had stocked the place with frozen ready-made meals and veggie packs and long-life milk and juice. Until the crisis had unfolded, he and Dillon had spent months communicating by notes, arguing over whose turn it was to do chores.

Sean microwaved a meal and carried it out onto his balcony. The summer night was balmy, and a breeze kept the insects at bay. He studied the stars that came and went beyond scuttling clouds and pondered the empty nights ahead.

So many triumphs had begun in this place, so much sorrow. He could see a light in Carey's kitchen and wondered if she was handling the breakup any better than Dillon. They were a perfect match in so many ways, and yet wrong in all the others.

Which pretty much summed up Sean's love life as well.

He finished his meal, pushed his chair away from the table, leaned back, and asked the stars how he was going to survive the vacant hours. His life since he'd learned to transit had been a headlong rush into one roller-coaster thrill after another. Even his awful days at the awful Diplomatic school had been crushingly full.

Everything that had come before—his empty home and now-divorced parents, the agonies of high school, the teenage boundaries that had ruled and limited his existence—all of that was gone now. Replaced by a realm containing a hundred and nineteen known worlds. Only now . . .

Defeated by the future void, Sean rose from his chair and went inside. As he stretched out and turned off the light, his gaze repeatedly fell upon Dillon's empty bed. His lonely frustrations blanketed him. He could not shake the sense that his life was over.

He was three months shy of his twentieth birthday.

21

Dillon's instruction as an interstellar spy consisted of one night's language training and a fifteen-minute warning. Most of the cautionary period was spent trying to land a date. And failing.

His transition from prisoner to secret agent was handled by Advocate Cylian and a senior Messenger. The Advocate booked him into quarters used by administrative types stationed on Serena for some temporary duty. Dillon had a very nice hotel suite with a mini kitchen, but it still felt like a barracks. He ate in the main hall and returned to his chambers, exhausted from the longest day of his life. Then he remembered to put on the language crown Cylian had left for him. At least that was familiar enough. He snapped it open, fitted it on so the communication jewel resided over the center of his forehead, and collapsed into bed.

The next morning, Cylian escorted Dillon to her office and

apartment. They transited into both several times, until she was certain he had them well established as emergency links.

Cylian doubted very much that Dillon would survive, and told him so repeatedly.

The senior Messenger who accompanied them was named Aldo. He was assigned as Dillon's link to his new destination. Aldo clearly considered Dillon competition for Cylian's attention, which was pretty amusing, since she showed them both the same frosty attitude. But Dillon only needed to smile in Cylian's general direction for Aldo to get all red in the face. The guy was snotty, vain, and beanpole thin. He wore a tailored uniform with what appeared to be real gold buttons. His brown hair was a rat's nest that probably required an hour in front of the mirror and a quart of wax to get just right.

"All of this is a terrible mistake," Cylian repeatedly told Dillon. "If I had my way, we'd take at least a few months and train you properly in all manners of tradecraft."

The word carried electric appeal. Tradecraft. He asked, "You'd like to play instructor?"

She was an inch or so shorter than he was, and trim in a manner that only heightened her feminine curves. Her icy attitude was now spiced by fretful concern. "It's such a shame you won't live to study with anybody."

Aldo offered a sniff of derision. "At least this one is expendable."

The Advocate dismissed the guy with a single frigid glance. Then she caught sight of Dillon's grin and narrowed her gaze even further. "Rightly or wrongly, my superiors believe your frontier-world upbringing has instilled an ability to adapt to the unknown and survive. I only wish I could agree with them."

"So what reward do I get for proving you wrong?"

"Pay attention, please. We can't supply you with false papers or even a decent reason for being there. The situation is too fluid, the planet too chaotic. All we have are rumors of a weapon capable of cutting through a warrior's strongest shield."

That got his full attention. "Wait, you mean some humans have harnessed the aliens' power of attack?"

"We have no idea."

"Why would they even want to do that?"

"Which precisely is the reason I have argued against your being inserted. We simply do not know enough."

"What *do* you know?"

"Very little. And I am strictly forbidden to discuss the suspicions that have raised so many alarms." She clearly disliked that intensely.

Dillon, however, found things falling into place. "Makes sense."

"Excuse me?"

"They don't want me to go in with preconceived notions. Smart."

She cocked her head to one side, causing her raven hair to spill over one shoulder like a dark frost. "Which is precisely what my superiors have been saying."

"And they're right."

She and the Messenger both scrutinized him now. Finally

Cylian said, "Find this weapon, if it exists. Buy or steal one if you can. And get out."

"If I survive," Dillon added for her.

"You are headed into a merchant's compound on a mining world. In truth, it is little more than a pirate stronghold. There is no recognized law, no order, not even a real government. Each territory is at war with all the others. Alliances are fluid and highly unstable." Her voice grew increasingly strident. "I urge you to refuse this assignment."

"What would you think of me if I turned and ran?"

Her gaze carried the force of an ink-dark laser. "I would think, 'There goes a man who will breathe his way through another hour.'"

22

Dillon's transit point was the eye of a hurricane.

The Messenger brought them into the main room of what might have been a large storage hut. All the windows were barred and shuttered. Dillon crept over to the massive double doors and peered through a spyhole. He could see snatches of a broad patio covered by a striped awning. A few sheets of paper were scattered about the floor, along with some lengths of twine, a pair of overturned chairs, three lanterns, and a pile of boxes. Otherwise, nothing.

He shifted to another window and saw bedlam on all sides, people running and screaming and the sounds of clashing metal. Dillon wondered at the absence of bombs or guns, but not for long, because there came a sound he had learned to recognize at the Academy. A brief, searing crackle was followed by the stench of a lightning strike, which meant someone was firing an energy weapon. The crowd only surged and screamed all the more.

The Messenger had told Dillon very little about their destination. Their primary contact was a merchant in a disputed territory. The man dealt mainly in carpets but was also a conduit for black market goods. How the merchant had been contacted by the alliance, the Messenger had no idea.

Aldo was typical of most Messengers. They were educated and cultured and utterly unaccustomed to danger. They loathed Dillon for the way he seemed to enjoy peril. What he felt really wasn't enjoyment, however. Whenever faced with real hazards, Dillon simply came into his own.

Aldo remained frozen in the position of his arrival. Then the energy weapon fired again, only this time it carved a hole through the wall beside the main doors. Another few inches to the left and the Messenger would have been headless. Dillon scrambled over and plucked the officer's legs from under him. Aldo hit the stone floor hard.

"Stay down." Dillon waited long enough to ensure the man did not rise, then crawled back to the side window. He risked a glance, then shifted back to the spyhole. "The crowds are thinning. Looks like the assault is easing . . ."

Dillon stopped in mid-sentence because a woman suddenly transited into the hut. She was scarcely more than a girl, a blonde-haired wispy thing. He thought she looked like a street waif, with pale eyes that showed neither surprise nor mercy. She carefully surveyed them and the room. In the hut's meager light Dillon saw how she checked them for weapons, took in the Messenger's gaudy attire, and then dismissed them as holding no threat. It was only after she vanished that Dillon realized her tan coverall was perhaps a uniform.

From where he sprawled on the floor, Aldo gasped, "There are no transiters in this system!"

Dillon had to laugh. The guy had finally offered him one bit of intel, and it was totally wrong. Dillon crawled over and crouched down beside the Messenger. One look into his terror-stricken gaze was enough to know he was a liability. "Okay, Aldo. Now's the time you tell me why we're here."

"She, the Advocate—"

"Not here on this planet. This room. You said your contact was a merchant, right?"

"Carpets, yes. But he also dealt in intel."

"How did he make contact with the system?"

"There was another Praetorian Guard."

The way he spoke left Dillon certain. "He's dead, right? The guard."

"Vanished."

Which was the same thing, most likely. "Let me guess. Your group set the guard up here with a lot of gold, and he came buying intel, which this particular merchant offered to supply."

"How did you know?"

Dillon didn't bother responding. He assumed one of the merchant's own group probably sold out the guardsman. All it would have taken in a lawless world was one word in the wrong ear about a lone guy walking around asking the wrong questions and carrying gold. The killers probably lined up down the street.

Which meant the Advocate was probably right about his chances of survival.

But there was nothing to be gained from telling this to the Messenger. Aldo was already scared enough.

"Look around. Your contact must have known something was going down. The place is totally empty." Dillon gripped the guy's shoulder and heaved him to a seated position. "So maybe he'll come back. But right now I need you to leave."

"I . . . What?"

"Go. Head out. You got me here. Your job is done."

"I don't . . . You're *staying?*"

Dillon thought the guy's astonishment was almost comic. "Didn't you hear Cylian? Somebody thinks this is important enough to risk my life."

Aldo looked ready to argue. Then the dusty air was rent by a high-pitched scream. He winced, then cried, "Come with me!"

"Not on your life." Which Dillon thought was good for another quick grin. "Have a good trip."

Aldo started to argue, then seemed to think better of it and vanished.

Dillon crawled back to the window facing the main avenue. The hut was fronted by a broad display area that stretched out to meet the avenue. The streets he could see were almost empty now. He spotted a few furtive heads that appeared and then swiftly vanished. He suddenly realized he had a raging thirst, strong enough to tempt him to open the doors and go in search of a frosty mug.

Then the tiny young woman in uniform transited back into

the hut. She was accompanied by a much larger guy, this one holding a weapon Dillon did not recognize. A rifle of some sort. The guy held it like he knew his business.

The woman spoke in a throaty whisper, her voice like her eyes, belonging to somebody much older. "You want to live, yes?"

"Absolutely."

"Tell us why you are here."

Dillon hesitated, which only caused the man to lift his gun and take a more careful aim.

He decided it was time to throw the dice. Gamble with a life that some people thought was down to its last few puffs.

He transited from one side of the room to the other. Then back. Again. A third time, only faster.

The pair watched in open-mouthed astonishment.

"I've come looking for you guys," Dillon told them. "Take me to your leader."

23

Dillon transited with the scrawny young woman and the trooper to a balcony perched to one side of a giant stone cube. When they arrived, she released them both and slid down the banister like a professional dancer. Or a thief. The guard ordered Dillon to descend the stairs in a more orthodox manner.

Dillon took his time, studying what he assumed was a battlefield garrison HQ. It had the orderly bedlam of a tight and efficient troop. He watched a transit team arrive with a clutch of prisoners whose terror-stricken expressions suggested they had no idea what had just happened to them. Which was interesting, as it suggested a world where transiting was unknown. He had to assume this was an outpost world. But if so, how did a military group form itself around a transit squad?

The lumpish guard pointed him to a spot directly below the balcony. A stone guardrail ran down the room's center.

The chamber reminded Dillon of a police station. The guard watched him carefully but kept his weapon pointed at his feet.

"Where are we?" Dillon asked.

"We wait for the commander." The guard held up a hand to Dillon's next question. "He asks the questions, not you."

The warning carried no heat, so Dillon said, "Okeydokey." And went back to rubbernecking.

The room was maybe sixty feet to a side. The shuttered windows were set along one wall that also contained broad double doors. The high ceiling and walls and floor were all carved from the same porous stone, more grey than yellow but pleasant to look at. Dillon wondered if the room had started life as a cave, for the corners were not completely symmetrical and the ceiling light-fixtures dangled from what appeared to be stumps of stalactite.

He asked the guard, "Are we underground?"

"We are indeed, good sir, and you must thank your lucky stars that's the case. For this planet has no atmosphere of its own. None whatsoever!" The man who approached was only slightly older than Dillon, and despite his dusty and unkempt appearance, he carried himself with the air of a prince. He had flashing grey eyes and hair more russet than red. "Are you from the Human Assembly?"

"Sort of."

"What a grand response! 'Sort of.' I take it you are not the Assembly's official Examiner?"

"I'm a lieutenant with the Praetorian Guard," Dillon replied. "Sort of."

"I positively adore a man who can bend his words! Flavor

and nuance are essentials to surviving tight spaces and wooing ladies, no?"

"Absolutely," Dillon replied, liking the man already. "I'm Dillon."

"And I am Vance. An honor to meet you." He gave a courtly bow. "What sort of capacity brings you here to our corner of Aldwyn?"

The crowd that had grown around them consisted of young faces, none older than the officer who addressed him. Most were grinning, save for the girl who had brought him here and a taller woman now standing beside her. The woman's cautious intelligence, her taut awareness, and the way the others gave her space suggested to Dillon that here stood another officer. She was also quite attractive, if one liked their ladies as beautiful as a polished blade.

Dillon did not respond to Vance, because the crowd parted and the team's leader stepped forward. There was no question as to who Dillon now faced. He was no older than any of the others. But he carried himself with the bitter strength of a man either born or determined to rule. Dillon doubted the officer had slept in days.

The man nodded a greeting to Vance and asked, "What have you learned?"

"His name is Dillon, he's with the Praetorian Guard, and he's an unofficial representative of the Assembly. Sort of." Not even his superior officer's presence could stifle Vance's affable good cheer. He said to Dillon, "Allow me the distinct pleasure of introducing Commander Logan. And this is my fellow officer, Subaltern Nicolette."

RENEGADES

Logan demanded, "How do you come to speak our language?"

"We're prepped in advance of all landings, sir."

"In what way?"

As Dillon opened his belt pouch, both Vance and the guard stepped in front of their commander. Dillon liked that, how they instinctively protected their chief, even if it meant risking their own safety. He slowly extracted the small case, opened the lid, and unfolded the device. "It's called a language headset. You wear it while you're asleep."

Logan accepted the device, inspected it briefly, then handed it back. "How do you know your superiors won't indoctrinate you with something other than a new tongue?"

Dillon folded the device and slipped it back into the box. "You don't."

"A dangerous implement," Vance said.

"Almost as risky as transiting," Dillon replied.

"As what?"

"Transiting. What we did to get here."

Logan and his officer exchanged looks. "We call it ghostwalking."

"I like that name," Dillon said. "A lot."

Nicolette stepped up to Logan's other side and asked Dillon, "Why are you here?"

"I'm a spy."

Logan's smile transformed his features, erasing the harshness, at least for a moment. "Should you be telling me this?"

"Not if you're my enemy," Dillon replied. "But I'm pretty sure you're not."

Logan seemed to find that amusing as well. "Explain your-self."

"I've been sent here to find a weapon."

"What sort?"

"I have no specifics. We don't even know if it actually exists."

"This 'we' being the Praetorian Guard," Logan said.

"Right."

Vance offered, "It must be quite a device, to have the Prae-torian Guard send a spy."

"It is," Dillon assured him. "If it exists."

"Describe it," Logan ordered.

"I was specifically not given details, because nothing con-crete is known. But the rumors suggest it has the capacity to break through the shields that transiters create with the same energy they use to shift from place to place." Their lack of surprise made him ask, "You can do this too?"

Nicolette demanded, "Why does this surprise you?"

"It's just . . . we were told no one in this system could transit—ghost-walk."

Their mirth was shared by all. Logan asked, "This transit energy can also be developed as a weapon?"

Dillon thought the guarded manner of their gazes sug-gested they already knew the answer. "Many different weapons."

Logan asked, "You will show us?"

Though it would mean breaking about a dozen regs, Dil-lon did not hesitate. "Absolutely."

Vance asked, "And what if we were to tell you that we possess the weapon your Praetorians seek?"

"Then I'm a dead man," Dillon said, and matched his smile.

Logan asked, "So a rumor of this weapon brought you here to this wandering planet."

"The merchant's hut where your squad found me—he was a spy for the Assembly. He claimed the weapon exists and offered enough evidence to raise the alarms. Why did your squad enter that hut, by the way?"

"The squad clearing the area found a group of our foes gathered outside," Vance replied, then pointed to the thin woman. "Sidra checked it out."

The commander was clearly unimpressed. "You have been sent on a fool's errand."

"What makes you say that, sir?"

Vance replied, "Because ghost-walking has not existed in this system for over a thousand years."

Nicolette added, "Long enough for ghost-walkers to become legends. Most people do not believe they ever existed."

Which explained the prisoners' terrified expressions. "And yet here you are," Dillon said.

Both officers glanced at Logan, who replied, "Even so, there is no use for such a weapon as you describe."

Dillon asked, "Mind if I stick around, you know, just in case?"

"You are wasting your time," Logan replied. "Will there be more like you?"

"Not unless you want," Dillon replied. "Not unless you invite them."

"Which I most certainly do not. Is that clear?"

"Crystal. Sir."

Logan inspected him with an officer's gaze, probing far beneath the skin. "Why should I trust you?"

"I've been completely honest with you," Dillon replied. "And who knows? I may be able to offer some support."

"Then you may stay, under two conditions. First, you remain under guard at all times, and do not ghost-walk unless given express permission."

"Agreed," Dillon said.

"And second, you teach my ghost-walkers your methods of combat."

24

Sean was awoken by the sound of a giant *BONG.*

For a single heart-stopping moment, he was back at the Academy, about to reenter the nightmare of arrest at the hand of interplanetary cops, there to drag him back to prison . . .

The second chime found him standing beside his bed, heart pounding and breath coming in tight gasps. He fought off the urge to transit to safety. He told himself he was free — the trial was over, the charges dropped.

A third *bong,* and the one-armed colonel who had introduced him and Dillon to transiting stood in the middle of his dining area.

Carver said, "I never thought I would see this place again."

Sean did his best to fit his heart back into its proper position. "What are you doing here?"

"That's precisely what I want to ask you."

"I got arrested," Sean replied. "And imprisoned. And put on trial. Or did you miss that news?"

"I missed nothing."

"Really nice of you to visit us, by the way."

"I was ordered to stay away," Carver replied.

"Who by?"

A second voice replied, "By me."

And there he was. Elenya's father, former Ambassador to the Lothian system, now a senior mover and shaker in the Assembly, stood beside Carver. Anyon grimaced as he surveyed the loft. "I had forgotten how this place is so . . ."

Sean cut him off with, "Homelike. Cozy. Welcoming. At least to the people who belong here."

Anyon sighed but did not rise to the bait.

Sean decided whatever it was that had brought them here required pants. He said to Carver, "Make coffee. Give me five minutes."

Sean carried his ire and a change of clothes into the bathroom. He tried to tell himself that the Ambassador had ample reason to dislike his home. Anyon's daughter had fallen in love with an off-worlder here in this loft. And then she had offered to divorce her family when Anyon and his wife had tried to pry them apart. Only now Elenya was gone. And confronting the Ambassador's disdain only rubbed salt in Sean's open wound.

He took his time showering and shaving and dressing. But his anger only strengthened with each passing minute. Anyon and his wife had detested Sean's relationship with their daughter from day one. Sean had long suspected their opposition had played a major role in driving Elenya away.

And then there was the other issue—how Anyon had wanted to erase Sean's and Dillon's memories. Steal from them the very concept of transiting. And all the worlds they had come to know, all the adventures, his every memory of loving Elenya.

Sean brushed his hair, tucked in his shirt, and decided it wasn't all bad, Anyon showing up like this. Truth be told, what Sean needed most on this foul day was a quarrel.

But when he emerged from the bathroom, Anyon disarmed him with just four words. "We need your help."

Sean was surprised enough to confess, "Of everything I might have expected to hear from you, that doesn't make the list."

"Our need is desperate," Carver added. He and Anyon were seated at the dining table directly below the skylight. Carver indicated a steaming mug and a plate with dried fruit and cheese set by the empty chair next to his. "Come join us."

"Forgive me for arriving unannounced and now launching straight in," Anyon said. "But time is of the essence."

"Anyon has just been appointed planetary Ambassador to Cygneus Prime," Carver explained. "He is taking Ambassador Kaviti's place and is due at the opening ceremonies in less than four hours."

Sean opted for a chair on the other side of the table. He slid the mug and plate over in front of him. "Cygneus is a renegade system."

"They were," Anyon said. "And the fact that you paid attention to your lessons helps us immensely."

"Six months ago, they formally requested to join the Assembly," Carver said. "After refusing our envoys the right to even visit for centuries."

"Their request arrived precisely when our sources began sending us rumors of a new weapon," Anyon continued. "One with the capacity to break through the Praetorian shields."

"I thought that was something only the aliens could manage," Sean said.

"So we claim," Carver said, as grim as Sean had ever seen him. "But there are legends from our distant past of weapons that could carve right through our strongest defenses, and armor that deflected every Praetorian means of attack."

Sean saw the unspoken message on both men's faces. "These weapons came from the Cygneus system?"

"Dragon blades, they were called," Carver said. "Wielded by a group known as Assassins."

"They were not just legends," Anyon said. "I have studied the records. The threat was very real. But it remained only within the Cygneus system. And they wanted nothing to do with the Assembly."

"Until now," Carver said.

Sean looked from one man to the other. "There's more, isn't there?"

"The group who tried to have you imprisoned is seeking to quash these very same rumors," Anyon said.

"But why?"

"We have no idea."

Carver amended, "Actually, some of us think —"

"We will not cloud this discussion with unfounded theories," Anyon said.

Carver sighed and went silent.

Anyon went on, "We are here because Dillon has been sent to seek out evidence of these weapons. We thought there was a support group in place to assist him. But our guardsman has vanished, along with the merchant who was our source of intelligence. And the Messenger who formed our link to this crew claims he and Dillon arrived in the midst of a pitched battle."

Sean finished his meal in thoughtful silence. He pushed his plate aside, drained his mug, and said, "You want me to go help Dillon."

"What I want," Anyon replied, "is for you to become an official member of my staff."

While Sean digested that, Anyon declared, "Whatever you decide, you are hereby graduated from the Academy." He gestured. "Colonel, if you please."

Carver slipped a heavily embossed envelope from his pocket and offered it to Sean. The packet was sealed with the Academy's gold stamp. "Congratulations. You are hereby welcomed to the ranks of Diplomats."

"Junior ranks," Anyon corrected. "Most new graduates are expected to serve within the bureaucratic system for several years."

Sean resisted the urge to tell them to skip the windup and get to the pitch. He decided whatever Dillon had going on, it could wait a while longer. "I've tried serving you people, and look where it got me."

Carver said, "You will address your superior in the proper fashion."

"See, that's where you both have it all wrong. I'm not his subordinate. If whatever you're leading toward requires that attitude, you can bounce on out of here. Because this conversation is permanently over."

The bald statement and the calm way Sean spoke silenced them both. Anyon was the first to recover. "It is precisely this attitude that may serve us well."

"There's that word again," Sean said. "Serve."

Anyon chose to ignore his reply. "We represent the same cause as Commander Taunton."

"This cause," Sean said. "Does it have a name?"

Carver replied, "We call ourselves Allies."

"And the bad guys?"

"Officially, they do not exist," Carver reminded him. "But we've heard that they call themselves the Order of the Scepter. A scepter is a staff held by an emperor as a sign of his authority. Sort of an ornamental weapon."

Sean protested, "But the Human Assembly has no emperor."

His words made the two older men become grimmer still. Finally Anyon said, "You are hereby assigned a place in the Institute of Higher Learning."

"The youngest ever," Carver added. When Sean remained silent, Carver said, "A word of thanks is in order."

But Sean was still trying to get used to the idea of having

shifted from a rudderless existence to being counted among the Assembly's elite cadre. Incoming Institute cadets carried the official rank of major.

Anyon said, "It is customary for a new member of the Institute to serve under the guidance of a senior Diplomat."

Sean had heard of this. "My official sponsor."

"In your case, you had three," Carver said. "Insgar, myself, and the Ambassador here."

This time, Sean had no choice but to say, "Thank you both."

Anyon might have smiled. Sean did not know him well enough to tell the difference between a smirk and genuine mirth. "Your brother is on Aldwyn, a mining planet in the Cygneus system."

"Aldwyn is a phenomenon known as a wandering planet." Carver waved that aside. "Everything else must wait. The Ambassador has to prepare."

Anyon continued, "You will be installed as a member of the official cadre responsible for determining whether the system is ready for admission to the Assembly. Your official title is Junior Planetary Examiner."

Now Sean could think of nothing to say except, "Wow."

"You will journey with my team initially. Once your credentials are well established, you will transit to Aldwyn and coordinate with your brother. Cylian and I will be your contacts." Carver handed over a palm-size tablet. "This contains an outline of your official duties. There is also a summary of what little we know about the situation on Aldwyn. Its capital is called Loghir. You are formally charged with making an initial survey. Your official remit allows you entry to any place at any time. You are required to travel without guide or monitor."

Anyon said, "You must locate your brother as swiftly as possible. The Messenger's name is Aldo. He will serve as your point of entry. Report back as soon as you can."

"Take great care," Carver said. "Aldwyn's other name is the Dead World. From all accounts, the planet deserves its reputation."

25

The corporal guard's name was Kyle, and he proved to be a nice guy, once the officers decided Dillon was no threat. Sidra shadowed them but did not speak to Dillon at all. The pair took him to the mess hall, where he ate a meal as good as many he'd known at the Academy. While he ate, Kyle told him, "I was a corporal in the supply depot. All my future held was eight more years of sheer boredom. No chance of any real duties." He pointed to his left knee. Dillon had already noticed how he slightly dragged his leg with each step. "Had this since birth."

"But they drafted you anyway?"

"Oh, no. I enlisted. It was my ticket out. At least at the supply depot I ate well. Most of my unit share two traits— hard beginnings and a desire to better ourselves."

"How did you come together?"

"Through Logan," Kyle replied. "So he should be the one to explain."

Thankfully, it was approaching their downtime, because Dillon was at the end of a very long day. He was assigned a bunk in a barracks with about a dozen male troopers. He had intended to stay awake and see what useful items might arise during the lights-off chatter. But he was asleep the instant his head hit the pillow.

The next morning they breakfasted in the mess, then waited in the front room for orders. Dillon saw another squad arrive with four new prisoners in tow. The captives were ushered back through a side door, which opened long enough for him to spy a trio of holding cages.

Logan's leash proved both long and flexible. First Vance and then Nicolette took Dillon on forays into the market area. They clearly enjoyed watching Dillon's reaction to his first sight of a crystal dome. A river of silver formed a pendant across the black sea.

The market held a tawdry, careworn air. It reminded Dillon of stories he'd read about the Marrakech casbah, the sort of place tourists might come looking for trouble, and find it. He imagined that when the place was in full swing, almost anything could be had for a price, including the buyer's own limbs. Dillon thought the vast cavern held an almost irresistible appeal.

They showed him the guarded tunnel leading to Clan Havoc's main holds. They explained the wandering planet's unique history. When Logan joined them at a restaurant for bowls of some unnamed stew, Dillon asked, "How did you find the walkers?"

Logan finished his bowl and asked for tea. He then turned

back to Dillon and waited. There were five of them at the table—Logan, Dillon, Kyle, Nicolette, and Sidra. Dillon ate and waited with them. The stew tasted good, a lot better than many of the meals he'd eaten at the Academy. Of course, he was on an airless planet and had seen no area set aside for growing real food. Dillon could see the headline now: *Former Praetorian cadet, recently released from prison, dies on secret mission after eating rat stew spiced with tunnel fungus.*

Then he realized Logan was waiting for him to answer his own question. Dillon said, "There's a specialist division of transiters called Watchers. One of the abilities that all senior personnel must learn is how to detect a potential transiter, even when the individual doesn't know they hold the gift. That's how we were found."

Nicolette asked, "We?"

"I have a twin brother. Sean."

"He walks the ghost paths as well?"

The ghost paths. Dillon loved how that sounded. "He does."

"How many specialties for the walkers are there?"

"A lot. But they break down into six main groups. Admin, Instructors, Messengers, Watchers, Diplomats, and Praetorian."

Nicolette continued to play interrogator, allowing Logan to sit back, sip his tea, and observe. "No merchants?"

"That would put us into direct conflict with planetary interests," he replied, giving them the party line. "Some transiters disagree. But that's the status quo for now."

"All of you develop weaponry?"

"Just Praetorians. The planetary Assembly likes to pretend we don't exist."

Logan cradled his mug and said, "To answer your question, I sniffed out the ghost-walkers. As you said, it happened before they knew it was even possible."

Dillon nodded. "With training, you can learn to sniff from half a world away."

"Even when I can't ghost-walk myself?"

He shrugged. "Everybody has abilities that come easy, others that only surface after a lot of work. My guess is, a few months of intense instruction and you'll develop that ability as well."

"I would like that," Logan said. "A great deal."

Dillon's next question was interrupted by Vance rushing into the stall. "You need to come right now!"

Logan rose from the table and told Kyle, "Take our guest for another sortie."

"No, no," Vance protested. "He must come as well."

"What are you saying?"

He pointed back toward their temporary headquarters. "A prisoner just confirmed the weapon Dillon seeks is real."

26

Once Anyon departed from Sean's apartment, Carver asked, "Do you have something appropriate to wear?"

"Yes," Sean replied.

"The Institute's uniform won't work," Carver insisted. "You have risen beyond that. And not something that will tag you as originating from an outpost world. There are some among the Ambassador's party who'll be looking for a reason to dismiss a newcomer."

The more things changed, Sean reflected, the more they stayed exactly the same. He reached toward the back of his closet and extracted an outfit he had only worn once before. "Will this do?"

Carver's eyes widened. "Where did you come up with that?"

"It was Insgar's idea." The suit was an elegant copy of the senior Diplomat's formal attire. Only this one held neither medals nor rank. His jacket and trousers were both of midnight blue, tailored from the finest cloth available. The velvet collar was of the same color and matched the column hiding his jacket buttons. "I wore it to the dinner she held for Elenya's parents."

"That will do perfectly." As Sean changed, he said, "You know the story of the outpost twins who saved the Assembly?"

"Professor Kaviti claimed it was a trifling affair and refused to teach it," Sean replied.

"Ambassador Kaviti is a fool," Carver said.

"No argument there."

"When this is over, I will personally instruct you and Dillon in the matter. For the moment, know this. Your actions in defeating the aliens and the rescue of your friend's relative— both indicate that same potential." Carver gave that a long beat, then asked, "Do you know the definition of a hero?"

"No sir."

"A hero is a common soul who rises to meet the challenges of his or her time. I urge you to think on that." Carver rose to his feet. "Ready?"

"Yes," Sean replied. And now he was.

* * *

They made Sean stay with the official group through an excruciatingly long day. First came speeches in a language he had not yet had a chance to learn. Four hours spent sitting and trying not to fidget or yawn. Then Anyon and a potentate from Cygneus Prime signed some documents. Which meant another hour of standing around and applauding on cue. Then a press conference. Military parade. And finally a banquet. Sean had no idea what the planet looked like, other than some fancy rooms and the view from a balcony where he stood and watched an army march past.

The food at the banquet wasn't bad. At least, Sean enjoyed the first seven courses. After that, he kept hoping one of the servants would offer him a pillow. He was seated at the far corner of the central table, beside the same Cygnean official who had shadowed him all day. The guy didn't speak any lingo but his own, was about five hundred years old, had the face of a desiccated prune, and possessed all the personality of a cadaver.

After the banquet, Cylian stepped up beside him and said, "One more meeting and we're done."

Sean groaned softly.

"I take it you did not enjoy yourself."

"If this is a Diplomat's life," Sean replied, "you can count me out."

Only then did he realize she was smiling. It transformed her features. The cold hardness was completely erased. In its place was an elfin mischief. "This shouldn't take long," she promised.

But she was wrong. They met in Anyon's palace suite and went over the next day's schedule, which was basically more of the same. Nobody else seemed the least troubled by the prospect. When they finally broke up, Cylian motioned for him to remain behind.

After everyone except Carver departed, Anyon said, "Are you ready to begin your true work?"

"Absolutely," Sean replied.

"Our Sean did not enjoy himself today," Cylian offered.

"This is merely window dressing," Carver said. "Theatrics required by the job."

Anyon moved about the room, shifting the position of small items, then stepping to the next table. "I am wondering if it might be better to send in a bevy of Praetorians."

"No," Carver said. "No troops. Not yet."

"We don't even know if his brother is still alive."

Suddenly Sean was no longer sleepy. "What?"

"Dillon was supposed to have checked in," Carver said, then continued to Anyon, "There are a hundred reasons for him not having reported back. That is why we selected him as our field agent. A good agent must be able to live beyond the rules."

Anyon shifted to the window. "A dozen seasoned troops —"

" — will break the conditions being set in place by the treaty you are negotiating. We had to agree to that point before they issued our formal invitation."

Anyon shifted the curtains, stared at the night, then let the drapes fall back in place.

Carver turned to Sean and Cylian. He gestured silently. *Go.*

Cylian reached for his hand. They went.

27

Dillon thought the jail was the most cave-like portion of the entire militia enclosure. It was connected to the main headquarters building by a windowless rock corridor that extended between the rear hydroponics sheds. The barred enclosures filled a long, high-ceilinged room. Half of the cells were empty, which Dillon thought was curious, since so many prisoners had been brought through. He asked where the prisoners had been taken, but his guard replied that his question was not proper.

Dillon was beginning to spot the local transiters, or ghost-walkers, for they all shared the taut builds and hardfisted expressions of early poverty. As they passed through the jail, he saw how the caged prisoners shrank away at their approach, clearly terrified of being forced to walk the ghostly ways another time.

They had shifted the captive from the cages to a room that probably had belonged to a senior prison guard. It was windowless and whitewashed and became cramped when they all piled in—Dillon, Logan, Vance, Sidra, Nicolette, and the two soldiers who had been interrogating the prisoners before they were sent wherever.

The inmate looked like a nervous bank clerk, all except his hands, which were far too large for his scrawny frame. Dillon put his age at late forties in Earth years, and his weight at 120 soaking wet. Which this guy was definitely working toward, the way he was sweating. He was mostly bald, with two raccoon stripes of rat-brown hair running above each temple. He looked underfed and eager. Clearly the guy thought that this gathering meant he was one step closer to some kind of reward.

He wiped his nose every few words, like he had a nervous tic. His eyes burned like coals and were never still. Neither were his hands, big mallets that jerked and fluttered, like they fought against being attached to his gaunt arms.

Logan asked his questioners, "Does he speak our tongue?"

"Not a word, sir. Least, that's what he claims."

"Vance."

The gallant officer stepped forward and addressed him calmly. The guy's response was guttural and gunshot swift. Vance spoke again. The man barked in reply.

Vance turned to Logan and said, "He insists on seeing gold before he says anything else."

Nicolette said, "He had a blade hidden somewhere and tried to knife two of my crew when we brought him in. Let them have a few minutes alone and we'll see how fast he sings."

Logan shook his head. "We want the truth, not some carpet woven from Havoc lies." He turned to the interrogators and said, "Give me everything he's said so far. Word for word. Start from the beginning."

The woman who served as spokesperson for the pair was squat and had a pockmarked face. "We've been bringing them for the quick interrogations, one by one just like you ordered. Some are scared enough of the ghost-walk to tell us the little they know. Havoc is definitely planning a big push into Hawk territory. Duke Tiko is after claiming the Hawk province as his own."

"What we suspected," Nicolette said.

"Anything else?" Logan asked.

"Not until we started on this one. Soon as the door was shut and his mates couldn't hear, he claimed Havoc's been working on a new weapon. Something from long ago. Said Duke Tiko had a force training in secret. Just waiting for the right moment." She shrugged. "Then he demanded gold."

Logan turned to Vance. "If it's so secret, how does he even know it exists? Ask him that."

Vance used the same affable tone, and the guy responded with the same nervous snarl. "He claims to have been one of the early recruits to test the weapon. And that's all he'll say until the gold is in his hands."

"Tell the prisoner we will resume when payment is at hand." Logan said to the two guards, "You did well. This prisoner is to stay under constant watch."

"Aye, sir."

Logan waited until the prisoner had been led away, then

said to Dillon, "I could go to my contacts here and ask for their gold. We've done enough to justify their help, clearing most of the Havoc troops from the market. But my uncle is a cautious man. He will want to negotiate. It could require hours. Days. Plus, going to him means using up the debt they now owe me."

Dillon liked Logan's up-front manner. "I can get the gold here pronto."

But Logan wasn't done. "If I agree and let you return to your home planet . . ."

"Not my home," Dillon replied. "Serena. The capital of the Human Assembly."

"How do I know you won't return with a hundred of your Praetorians? I don't want your gold that much."

"I read you loud and clear," Dillon replied. "And I guess it all comes down to trust. But I have one thing I'd like to try that might just make my travel unnecessary."

28

Sean transited from the meeting with Anyon back to Cylian's office on Serena. Since she had left Kaviti's team she had been reassigned to another unit in the main judiciary building, one separated by several floors from Kaviti. She gave Sean long enough to anchor himself, then they transferred to her apartment.

Cylian's living quarters were surprisingly warm and feminine for such an aloof person. Sean did not know what to say about being there, and Cylian did not give him much of a chance. She handed him a language headset and bid him a good night.

Sean transited back to the loft and was asleep as soon as his head hit the pillow. The next morning, he took his time over breakfast, then had a long shower and dressed in jeans and an unironed knit shirt. As he hung the tailored outfit back in his closet, he stroked the sleeve, thinking back to the night in Insgar's compound—the dinner with Elenya and her parents and the love strong enough to defy planetary opposition. Or so Sean had thought.

He made himself another cup of coffee and drank it on the balcony. It was late afternoon Earth time, and the trees danced to an incoming summer storm. He returned inside, washed out the pot and his mug, then packed a bag.

As he prepared to transit back to Cylian's apartment, Dillon *blasted* into his consciousness.

During the aliens' first assault, Sean had developed an ability to communicate with Dillon by thought alone. It took them the better part of a year to get where they could control the process to a certain extent. But it never grew easy for either of them. Many within the transit community doubted they could do it at all, for the process had never been accomplished by anyone else. And now the emotions resulting from their unraveled relationships left them unable to do it at all.

Or so Sean had assumed.

Which magnified the shock of Dillon contacting him. The communication was fragmented but still carried the unmistakable sense of achievement.

. . . You there?

Sean leaned his head against the balcony door and concentrated as hard as he possibly could. The process required him to bond directly with the point in his gut where the transit force originated. He fashioned a terse reply, wrapped the energy around it, and sent back his own thought-bomb. *Talk to me.*

Dillon's message was tattered and unraveled around the edges.

. . . Use a little help here.

Where are you?

Dillon's response was just out of reach. It felt to Sean like he was trying to hear his brother over the howl of a mental hurricane.

He put everything he could into clamping a message into place, then shot out, *Say again.*

Aldwyn. Outer rim . . . Ask Cylian.

Sean asked because otherwise he wouldn't sleep nights. *Are you in danger?*

Dillon managed to add a chuckle to his frayed response. *No idea. Need gold.*

How much?

There was a long pause, then, *Call it fifty pounds. Coins.*

One of the remarkable oddities of the planets occupied by humans was the scarcity of certain elements. Gold was among them. More than half the planets had none at all. A hundred and nineteen systems, and gold remained one of the most precious commodities. It formed a language all its own.

Sean asked, *When and where?*

There was another pause. *My arrival point. Cylian knows. Ten hours.*

Sean both fashioned the response and spoke the words aloud. "On my way."

29

When Sean reported the contact with Dillon, Cylian needed a few moments to accept that an action she'd thought impossible had happened. Then she left and returned with Carver, whose own set of questions pretty much matched Cylian's.

Sean did not mind their interrogation, not even with the clock ticking in the background. He needed to fit his experience into the realm of possible. Carver then described for Cylian the events leading up to the alien invasion and the role those thought-bombs had played. She had heard it all before, but this was different. This was not some past improbability. This was now.

After Carver left to obtain the gold, Cylian insisted on preparing Sean and Aldo a meal. The senior Messenger who had deposited Dillon on the rogue planet was sent to her balcony. Cylian asked Sean to join her in the kitchen. She set him to washing and chopping vegetables, then said, "Your brother is a complete and utter rogue."

"No argument there," Sean replied. "Is that why you like him?"

"I never said . . ." She bit her lip. "You are every bit as much a rogue as he. Handsome adventurers with cavalier spirits."

"No one has ever called me handsome before," Sean said.

"It's true nonetheless." Her voice carried a new undercurrent, a soft music that rushed electric currents through his gut.

Sean asked, "How old are you?"

"Almost thirty in Serenese years."

Which made her twenty-four in Earth years. He said, "Dillon and I are twenty-five Serenese, almost twenty-six."

She stirred a sauce on the stove, her eyes fastened on her work. "You appear much older."

Abruptly Sean realized the discussion was no longer about Dillon. And Sean found it necessary to focus hard on the knife and the veggies. "Thanks, I guess."

"I am told high levels of danger and peril will do that," Cylian went on. "Not to mention a broken heart."

He turned around and stared at her back. "You know about Elenya?"

"I am now assigned to her father's staff. I made it my business to know." She paused, then asked, "Do you consider her a bad woman?"

He watched her reach into the shelves for a glass vial and sprinkle some spice into the sauce. A new fragrance filled the air, one he didn't recognize. "No. Causing a bad end to our relationship doesn't change her nature."

"Will you survive?"

"I don't understand the question. I'm here, aren't I?"

"Some strong people who are crushed by love, they see the world through rage and a need for vengeance on the innocents who pass their way."

Sean hesitated, then asked, "Is that what happened to you?"

When she turned around, he was half expecting to confront the frigid mask, the hyper-intelligence, the blank gaze. Instead, she said, "My story will come another time. If you like. Right now I am asking about you."

"The challenge is not to survive," Sean replied. "What I need to do is grow into something better."

The tip of her tongue emerged and touched her upper lip. But whatever she was about to say was halted by the Messenger entering the kitchen and demanding, "How much longer will you be? Whatever you're making smells both ready and fabulous, and I'm famished."

They ate on Cylian's veranda, a broad outdoor parlor that overlooked Serena's placid sea. During the meal, she and Aldo gave Sean an overview of the Cygneus system. They dined on a grain very similar to brown rice and vegetables cooked in a spicy sauce. When the table was cleared, Cylian asked if Sean had any questions.

"Most of what you've said, I already learned for class," Sean replied. "But I didn't mind hearing it a second time."

Carver arrived then, dressed in his formal Praetorian officer's uniform. He set a leather satchel on the veranda floor, listened as Cylian recapped their discussion, then said, "The Ambassador is waiting for me. The evening reception is under way." He nodded to Sean. "Stay safe. Return with the evidence we require." And he was gone.

The hour of their departure was fast approaching. Over a final mug of tea, the Messenger nervously described the chaos of their arrival. "Your brother was as calm as a seasoned general." He hesitated, then confessed, "I fell apart."

"The first time I was in a live-fire exercise," Sean replied, "I froze."

"I don't believe that," Cylian said. "Not for an instant."

"I lay flat on this massive pillar and tried to dig my fingernails into the stone," Sean recalled. "Dillon was singing. And laughing. I hated him."

"Your brother pushed me down and saved my life in the process," Aldo said. His smile was slightly canted. "I hated him as well."

As the final minutes counted down, Aldo started sweating so hard he stained his uniform collar. He fretted, "We don't even know if your brother is alive, and here we are risking another life, carrying more gold — "

"Give me a minute alone with Sean, please," Cylian said. When Aldo remained standing in her parlor, she walked over, gripped him by the arm, and led him back onto the veranda. She shut the door, swept drapes over the glass, then turned to Sean and declared softly, "Time is not our friend today."

He didn't know what to say to that.

She closed the distance between them. "I will be direct with you out of necessity. Your brother is nice, and I'm sure he is a very fine Praetorian. But he does not interest me. Not emotionally."

"Sure, I get that," Sean replied. "I figure Dillon does too. Flirting is just his way — " He stopped in mid-flow because she reached out and pressed one finger into the center of his chest.

"You, on the other hand, most certainly do."

Sean had no idea how to respond.

"I have been attracted to you since I watched you in court. Perhaps even before then. In the prison great room you were completely in charge of our conversation. Under such pressure, your freedom at stake, you defied the Assembly's might and made a mockery of Kaviti's authority."

Sean just stood there, a stone statue entitled *Man with Gaping Mouth*.

"I know Elenya personally," Cylian went on. "Would you like to hear why I think she left you?"

Sean managed a nod.

"She saw in you what I do. You are born to lead." Her voice lowered to a rich burr. "But I think Elenya wants to be the leader in her family. The *only* leader. She spent her early years fighting her father's authority. She did not want to play that same role in her own family. I don't think she realized this until your relationship began to mature."

Sean was close enough to see gold flecks in Cylian's smoky gaze. Close enough to catch a hint of some exotic fragrance. He managed, "What do *you* want in a relationship?"

She smiled, clearly approving of his question. She whispered, "Come back and find out."

Then she kissed him.

30

The arrival point was a dingy hut, empty now of everything but litter and Dillon and a small woman hiding in the shadows. Dillon greeted Sean with his patented lopsided grin. "Good to see you, bro."

"I brought your gold," Sean replied.

"I knew you'd come through." He pointed to the woman leaning against the back wall. "This is Sidra. She's one of the local ghost-walkers, which is their word for transiters."

Sean sketched a hello, then turned to Aldo and said, "Tell Cylian contact has been made. I'll be in touch as soon as there's something to report."

Dillon translated for Sidra, then told Sean, "It's important we only speak their tongue."

"Will do," Sean said. "Is there word of the weapon?"

"That's what the gold is for," Dillon replied. He waved a farewell to the Messenger, then asked, "Did they give you any trouble over the request?"

"We could have asked for ten times as much." Sean shared Dillon's grin. "Soon as I passed on your message, Carver bounced into high gear."

They transited to an almost empty market square. Only two of perhaps a dozen stalls were open. The seven intersecting lanes were all but void of life. Some doglike animal skittered across the stones, snarled at them, and disappeared.

Dillon gave Sean a moment to rubberneck, then pointed up. "Check this out."

Straight overhead was an empty void. An almost perfect circle, perhaps a quarter mile across, opened to a vast array of starlight. "Whoa."

"They say this planet survived its sun going nova," Dillon explained. "Blasted it from orbit and melted parts of the crust to diamond crystal maybe twenty feet thick."

Sean dragged his gaze away from the sky and studied the market. The ceiling was high enough to be considered a false sky. Strip lighting was embedded into the stone, long ribbons of palest gold. The market had to be five miles across. Bigger.

He asked, "That's what they mine here, diamonds?"

"Not that I know of." He nudged Sean. "Come on, Sidra's getting impatient."

"Just a second." Sean did not have any idea what was coming next. But he was fairly certain it would fling him into a fast-flowing rush of events. He did his best to ignore Sidra's presence and said, "It's about Cylian."

Dillon grinned again. "What, she's sent a message?"

"Not exactly." Sean swallowed. There was no telling how his brother would respond, given everything he'd been through on the romance front. "She's apparently into me. And the more time I spend with her, I think I'm into her as well."

Dillon studied him a moment, then asked, "What about Elenya?"

Sean nodded. That issue had dominated his thoughts since Cylian's farewell. "You and I both know it's definitely over."

"Roger that."

"Accepting it has been hard. And I don't know if I'm ready, you know . . ."

"For whatever comes next."

"Right." Telling his brother was harder than he had expected. Not because of Dillon. Because it meant accepting things himself. "But I want to try."

"With Cylian."

"Yes. Are you okay with that?"

Dillon's response was cut off by Sidra barking a laugh. "This twin of yours stole your woman?"

"He didn't steal, and she wasn't mine." Dillon kept his gaze on Sean. "Bro, if you think you can handle that one, go for it." He asked Sidra, "What's the worst kind of beast your planet has to offer?"

"Legends claim there once were dragons."

"Yeah, that sounds about right." Dillon's smile was slightly canted now. "You want to wrestle the mythical beast, she's all yours. You really think you can handle her?"

Sean let out a shaky breath. "Probably not."

31

hen Dillon offered to take the leather bag containing the gold, Sean did not object. Sean allowed himself to be swept along beneath a stone sky, down a central avenue broad as a six-lane highway. Their destination was a building set into the market's side wall, squat and solid as a bunker. Two troopers stood on relaxed guard by the massive double doors. Inside was a single vast room of stone and airy space. Sean wondered if the original builders designed their structures so large in order to ignore the fact that they lived permanently underground.

Within minutes of entering, they were surrounded by curious troopers. Sean tried to tell the difference between the so-called ghost-walkers and the regular soldiers, and failed. He took this as a very good sign. There was no sense of separation that he could detect, no superiority, no special status because of their singular gift.

Dillon drew him around with, "This is Commander Logan. My brother, Sean."

Logan demanded, "You understand our tongue?"

"Some. Yes sir."

The leader of Dillon's allies was scarcely older than Sean, mid-twenties at the most. But he bore a general's severity, calm and distant and constantly calculating. He was an inch or so taller than Sean, with a three-day growth over cavernous cheeks. His eyes were surrounded by plum-colored bruises. Logan looked as though he had not slept in weeks.

He asked Dillon, "You will let me try this language crown?"

"Whenever you like," Dillon said.

Logan nodded and said to Sean, "So you're the thinker. Does the fighter obey you?"

"Sometimes," Dillon said, continuing to play their spokesman. "When I have to."

Logan liked that enough to reveal an officer's smile. Tight, quick, and very angular. "You brought the gold?"

"Enough to make the satchel a burden." Dillon kicked the leather bag, and the coins inside clinked softly. "Somebody else can take it from here."

"So let's see what our turncoat has to offer," Logan said. As they headed for the back room, he added, "I like a man who guards his counsel. Welcome aboard."

* * *

Logan directed them into the office formerly belonging to the chief militia officer. When the gold was spread across the desk, Logan stepped back into the corridor and motioned for Dillon and Sean to stay inside the room. Isolated now with Sidra and his two officers, Logan said, "Tell me what you think."

Vance was uncharacteristically silent. Nicolette said, "I asked Dillon what his brother was like. He said people used to be unable to tell them apart. No longer."

Logan liked that. It indicated an honesty that went beyond simply fulfilling his duty to his allies. "Anything else?"

"I like the fighter," Nicolette admitted. "I was ready to dismiss him out of hand. But he has made himself part of the team."

Logan nodded, then asked Sidra, "Did they say anything I need to hear?"

She revealed a street urchin's laugh, raspy and edged by old pain. "The thinker has taken the fighter's woman."

"Tell me what they said, word for word."

When Sidra had related the exchange, Nicolette said, "They hide nothing."

Logan nodded again. He had been thinking the same thing. But Vance continued to frown. "Something bothering you?"

"You want to know if we should join with them when the battle starts."

Nicolette countered, "The battle is almost over. The market's ours."

Vance shook his head. "The turncoat's news changes everything."

"If what he says is true," Nicolette said.

"Confirming the rumors that brought the off-worlder here is warning enough," Logan said. He asked Vance, "Well?"

"I would have Dillon at my side. Willingly," Vance replied. "But the other? I think he is weak."

Nicolette said, "Dillon claims Sean is the better strategist."

Vance shrugged. "Thinkers hesitate. If we are facing a real enemy, that instant of hesitation could get us killed."

Nicolette studied the floor at her feet, then decided, "Give Vance the warrior. I will see if the thinker can also be a man of action."

Logan nodded. It was the response he had hoped for. He said to Vance, "Bring us the turncoat and let's see if the off-worlders' enemy is truly out there."

32

Dillon allowed himself to be separated from Sean, such that his brother was at the far end of the group. He liked having this opportunity to observe Sean. His brother was changing. Dillon had noticed it before, both in the prison and in the courtroom. But today was different. They were going into battle. Dillon had been certain of it from the instant he heard that a captive was willing to sell the information Dillon had been sent to obtain. He knew Sean would not shirk conflict. Yet he could also see that his brother was taking on the Diplomat's mantle of reserve. Sean was most comfortable with silence. He was the professional observer, the one who kept a tight rein until he had firmly established his compass heading. Dillon liked this, mostly because he knew he needed it.

Dillon lived for action. He liked the danger high. But he ran the risk of flying off in the wrong direction, lured by a false lead. He knew he could trust Sean to hold him back. He hoped the others would recognize this when the time came.

Sean asked, "This building was headquarters of the local constabulary?"

"Market militia, they're called," Nicolette replied.

"How many stayed to give battle?"

"Not a single solitary one," Logan replied.

"Scattered like rats, the lot," Nicolette said. "Why do you ask?"

"Were they under the pay of your foes, whatever they're called?"

"Clan Havoc," Logan replied. "And that is an excellent question."

There was a knock on the door, then Vance and a guard led in the prisoner. A metal band locked his wrists to his waist. The ends were linked to the guard's left arm.

Logan demanded, "Why do you have him chained so?"

"I suggested it," Vance said. "In case they had walkers of their own. Keep him anchored here. Maybe."

The man's dark gaze remained fastened on the glittering piles. "That lot's mine? All of it?"

"Unchain him, and station yourself by the door," Logan said to the guard, then pointed Vance into the empty chair on their side of the desk. "The gold is yours if you give us what we want."

The prisoner rubbed his freed wrists. "How do I know you'll keep your word?"

"What do they call you?"

"Pitt."

Nicolette snarled, "You will address the commander in proper fashion."

"Pitt, sir." His oversized hands were in constant motion. He tightened his belt, plucked at his coverall, stroked his wispy mustache, cracked his knuckles, pressed his temples, then went back to rubbing his wrists. He had an underfed look and a vicious air. He was, Dillon assumed, capable of anything for gold—or even for a good meal.

"My name is Logan, and I'm the senior survivor of the Hawk clan. You know a Hawk's word is his bond, yes?" Logan waited until the prisoner nodded. "So here is your choice, Pitt. You tell us everything you know. You satisfy our every question. Then you take this gold and we will plant you deep in Hawk territory, where you'll be guarded and kept safe until this engagement is finished. Then you and your gold are free to go wherever you like."

When the prisoner did not speak, Vance instructed with deadly ease, "Tell the commander you understand."

"I hear you, sir."

"If we are not satisfied with your responses," Logan said, "we will ship you back to Clan Havoc. And I assume you know what they do to turncoats."

"Make your last breaths hard, they do," Vance said. "Very hard indeed."

"No," Pitt said. "I'll talk."

And talk he did.

* * *

Sean listened with very real dread as the turncoat brought Anyon's and Carver's fears to life.

The Grey Assassins, Pitt called them. Giving flesh to legends over a thousand years old.

They numbered less than a dozen and were an unruly lot, he claimed. All of them were off-worlders, and most hated the need to follow orders. There had been fights between these off-world blades and Tiko's men. Only a few, but they had ended badly. Now most of the off-worlders had been moved back to wherever they came from. The leader of Clan Havoc had insisted that one of their elders be his permanent guest while the ditrinium was refined and their weapons constructed. The amount they required for their knives was staggering. A fistful was enough to power a military orbiter. Each knife had to be processed in a manner that took weeks. What was more, the uniform that gave these Assassins their name was woven with threads of yet more ditrinium. Duke Tiko had insisted that the cannons he had used to bring down the Cygnean battle fleet be built first, but the elder off-worlder had disagreed, and they had settled on one cannon, one uniform, one knife.

"This tale of yours has all the markings of barracks chatter," Logan declared, clearly goading the man.

Pitt bridled. Now that payment was agreed upon, he spoke the Hawk tongue with a rough twang. And he understood far more. "I ain't no liar," he snarled. "Any who says otherwise learns my skill with an Aldwyn blade. I'm a tunnel rat, born and bred. I don't hold no truck with empty words."

Logan glanced at Dillon and then back to Pitt. "So the trouble was shipped in from off-world, you say."

"Aye, that I did."

Dillon asked, "What is this he's saying about a battle fleet?"

"Clan Havoc defeated a full battalion sent from Cygneus Prime," Logan replied. He asked the twins, "You think these off-worlders he's speaking of come from beyond our own system?"

"Maybe," Sean replied. "Can I ask him something?"

"Have at it," Logan replied. "This appears to be your problem as well."

Sean asked Pitt, "Have you seen these off-worlders for yourself?"

"Only once," he admitted. "And that was from a safe distance. Tiko drew us up on parade, showing off his forces."

"What can you tell us about them?"

"The elders were dressed in uniforms of blue. Three, maybe four of them. All of an age, don't you know. Grey-haired or no hair at all."

"How long ago was that?"

Pitt's brow furrowed. "Three cycles, was it? No, four."

"Which would have made it around six months back," Dillon said.

Sean asked, "Does Havoc have ghost-walkers of their own?"

"Not on your life." Pitt smirked.

Nicolette demanded, "What strikes you as humorous?"

"The duke is right terrified of the prospect."

Logan leaned back. The twins were seated to either side of him. He looked first at Dillon, then Sean. Then back again.

Sean said, "So Duke Tiko knows the ghost-walkers exist."

"Oh, aye. He'd have to, wouldn't he. Seeing as how them

in blue come and go from his keep." Pitt took a step forward, another. His restless hands reached out and snagged a coin off the top of the pile. When no one objected, he took another and made them both disappear. "Made them off-worlders promise they'd not shift without his say-so. On account of the legends."

"Legends?" Sean asked.

Logan offered, "Havoc once ruled the largest continent on Cygneus Prime. Legend claims it was Havoc ghost-walkers who awoke the dragons. When the battle ended, Tiko's fore-bears scarcely had enough survivors to fill the holds of a single ship."

Sean asked, "How long ago was that?"

"More than twelve centuries," Nicolette replied. "Long enough for dragons to become part of the clan's legend, an excuse for their defeat."

"Eventually my Hawk clan took over the Havoc fief and ruled until they were defeated by the council that now rules Cygneus Prime," Logan went on. "Our own history is much more straightforward. We lost our fief in fair battle. But you hear such fables among many of the defeated clans. Their downfall came at the hands of those fell beasts. It is the only way their pride survived."

"Dragons," Dillon said. Just loving it.

Logan went on, "According to the legends, the dragons were finally conquered in a battle that laid waste much of our continent. The surviving dragons supposedly swore oaths of surrender and vanished. Swam into the inland sea at the heart of our former lands. They haven't been seen since."

"Because they never existed," Vance said. "Except to spice up the bedtime wonderings of children."

"Back to these so-called Assassins," Logan said to their captive. "What makes them special?"

"How they're equipped," Pitt said, more definite now. "Blades and uniforms made from ditrinium. All done up according to what the off-worlders say. Word is, they're wanting guns as well. But so far they haven't gotten one to work, not smaller than a fair-sized cannon. Something about the forging process makes it nigh on impossible to shrink the firing mechanism like the off-worlders want."

Logan turned to Sean and explained how it all came down to ditrinium. The metal found only on Aldwyn. Forged in the heat of a dying star. The mineral that powered Cygnean energy systems and the fleetest ships. Why the miners lived there at all.

When Logan went silent, Sean said, "The off-worlders aren't here to buy the mineral. They're after the finished goods."

Nicolette asked, "What does that tell you?"

It was Logan who replied, "The production was done in secret. For a purpose the off-worlders are so intent upon keeping to themselves, they give away the technology and pay to have it made here."

Dillon asked, "But who is the enemy?"

Sean nodded. That was the question. He asked Pitt, "What can you tell us about the weapons?"

"Long knives," the miner stated.

Vance said, "Knives don't explain this sort of secrecy."

Nicolette said, "You don't form a special brigade to carry knives."

"Knives long as my forearm," Pitt insisted. "And Tiko's new blast cannons, big as a fair-sized house they are, with di-trinium worked into their hearts. No shield can stand against them, is what we heard after your battalion went down."

Sean remained focused upon that first weapon. Knives. Tendrils of unease wrapped their way around his gut and squeezed, though he could not say for certain why, or what caused the unease.

Dillon's expression had turned as dour as Logan's. He said, "There's a faction among our group making trouble."

"You mean, walkers against walkers?" Logan asked.

"We don't know for certain."

"But we think that's the issue," Sean said. "And that's why we're here."

ᴣᴣ

oon after, Sean and Dillon were asked to leave the interrogation chamber. They exited and joined the ranks headed
toward the barracks mess hall. Sean was more worried than
tired, and he was very tired indeed. "What is the chance of
finding a bed around here?"

"Barracks," Dillon replied. "Pretty basic. I'll see about
getting you a bunk."

They collected plates and found spaces at one of the long
mess tables. They were not excluded from the general company, but not included either. Sean did not mind the isolation. He was still digesting everything Pitt had revealed when
Nicolette joined them.

"We're going to hold Pitt over a while," she said. "In case
we come up with more questions."

"He agreed?"

"We've moved him into an empty chamber. Guarded but
unchained." She waved away a trooper's offer to bring her a

meal. "We told him we needed time to set up his temporary haven, which is true enough. Logan is bringing over his uncle, Linux. He rules the Hawk fief on Aldwyn. Vance and I are dining with him tonight."

Sean asked, "You're bringing in reinforcements?"

"Logan thinks it's time to alert the local Hawk leaders. Whether or not we gain troops is up to Linux and his officers."

Sean saw the prospect of conflict pleased his brother, or at least excited him. Sean still felt the fear worms burrow in his own gut and pushed his plate aside.

Dillon said, "Know what strikes me most about today?"

Sean did not look up. "Yes."

Nicolette asked, "You can read his mind?"

"No." That was true enough. The rest could wait. "But I know him. And sometimes I know what he's thinking."

"So tell," Dillon said.

"Two things." Sean turned to the woman seated beside them. Nicolette was a striking woman in the fierce manner of a bird of prey. There was no soft component to her, from her gaze to the way her right hand curled around a weapon she did not hold. "None of your crew showed any interest in the gold for yourselves. Even though I suspect there are some former outlaws among your troops."

"Thieves and hard beginnings," she confirmed. "What does that tell you?"

"Troop loyalty," Dillon replied. "Strong officers. Great commander."

The mess hall's din was the only sound for a time, then Nicolette said, "And the second item?"

Dillon said, "Go on, bro. Tell the lady."

"I need to report back to my superiors," Sean said. "But first we've got to get inside that Havoc hold."

"You'll die," Nicolette said. "Slowly and not well."

"No he won't," Dillon said.

She glanced over at Sean's twin, then asked them both, "You have a plan?"

"That's what my brother is best at," Dillon replied. "Making plans."

34

ogan had no idea how Linux might feel about pomp and ceremony. In the end he decided to create as formal a structure as possible, given the circumstances. Linux was, after all, ruler of the last remaining Hawk fief.

They dined in the guard captain's private apartment, where a table had been discovered that had them all agog, for it was made of rare woods from Cygneus Prime's equatorial region. Deep red veins flowed through the table's polished surface like rivers in a wooden map.

Vance happily took charge of preparations. He enlisted three crew members who had served in the officers' mess and dressed them in clean coveralls. Four more soldiers were set as a formal guard by the entrance. Their meal was cooked by two who had trained as chefs. But the real prize had nothing to do with the food at all.

When Linux's transports halted in front of the former guard's station, Logan saluted his uncle and drew him through the kitchen, around the massive cast-iron stove, and into the pantry. The rear wall had been demolished, leaving behind a pile of rubble and yellow bricks. Vance led them down the secret stairwell, for he was the one who had insisted that such a chamber was bound to exist. Down and down they went, then into a series of four rooms with peaked ceilings and wall after wall of bottles.

Logan said, "There is another room beyond this one. The barred entrance was left open. All the shelves in that chamber were empty. I suspect it was reserved for wealth they took with them."

Linux took one flask down at random, wiped away the dust, and declared, "The captain lived well."

"He was your man?"

Linux shook his head. "His grandfather ruled the fief before we arrived. The father surrendered to us before the first drop of blood was shed. His one request was to be allowed to keep his troops intact and serve as market guards. I put some of my own men among them. Few cared for the duty, and those who did have vanished with the captain and his troops." He surveyed the shelves. "These bottles hold a king's ransom."

"It's yours," Logan said. "All of it. Take the lot."

Linux swiveled slowly around. His gaze was dark as an unlit tunnel.

Logan went on, "This and the missing treasures are drawn from your market."

"Some would say this was booty, yours by right of combat," Linux replied.

"Call it a gift of thanks for allowing me and my men this chance to prove ourselves."

Linux said slowly, "You remove the Havoc raiders from my market cavern. And now *you* thank *me*."

Logan waited.

Linux sighed. "I suppose you might as well give me the rest."

＊＊＊

With Linux were three grey-haired administrators, two women officers, and a bearded general. They shared their leader's worried silence. They asked few questions. Linux's gestures were small. Stillness suited him. He was, Logan decided, a cautious man who had adapted well to his world of caves and deep shadows.

Their meal consisted mostly of vegetables found growing in the militia's hydroponics gardens. It was plain fare, but no one minded. Linux and his band gave little indication they were aware of what they ate.

Logan had opted not to invite the twins. He was joined at the table by Nicolette and Vance only, and they all wore the same coveralls. Their simple clothing, without any sign of status or rank, was a direct contrast to the finery of Linux and his team.

Logan sensed the undercurrent of tension and knew the reason. His gift of the wine cellar's content had done nothing to ease Linux's nervousness. He and his crew awaited Logan's terms. Logan had effectively seized control of the market. He had shown the ability to halt the Havoc invasion, at least temporarily. Linux and his officers feared Logan's demands would tax them as severely as Havoc's raids. Perhaps worse.

Only Vance remained untouched by the tense mood, or at least he pretended better than any of the others. He kept up a light banter that Logan did not bother hearing.

Toward the end of the meal, Sidra popped into view. As Logan had requested, she saluted the table, but she could not completely hide her smirk. "Guard details have changed watch, Commander. All quiet. Havoc tunnel remains empty."

"Thank you."

When Sidra vanished, the table remained trapped in complete and utter astonishment. Finally Linux said, "So that's how you did it."

And in that instant, Logan had the answer to his unspoken question. He could see the same response in all their faces.

They were not going to help him.

Revealing his ghost-walkers and their secret ability changed nothing as far as Linux was concerned. He would remain cautious. Uncommitted. Because all they saw was the risk of another defeat.

Logan turned to Nicolette and said, "We need to decide about trusting the twins."

He could see Vance's confused frown. But Nicolette understood. At least, she was willing to follow his lead. "Everything Dillon has said rings true. He is a trained soldier. He will hold up in a fight. He cares for other troopers. He listens. Sean . . . he continues to surprise me." She hesitated, then added, "I like them both."

Linux asked, "Twins?"

"Ghost-walkers who seek to join us," Logan said tersely.

Nicolette went on, "Sean has developed a strategy we need to discuss."

When she cast a doubtful glance at their guests, Logan said, "Continue."

"There is a talent some of their highly trained ranks can do. Dillon calls it hunting. They extend their awareness." When Logan did not respond, she added, "Beyond their physical forms."

"Which one can do that?"

"Both have," Nicolette replied. "Under high-stress conditions. But their abilities have been restricted of late. Neither is certain it will be possible again."

Logan leaned back. "They want to hunt in Havoc territory."

"They want to try."

"What if Havoc has hunters of their own?"

"Sean is certain they do not." She shrugged. "You need to ask him. All I can say is, on this point he was confident."

Logan turned back to the group opposite him. "I asked you here to share with you our tactics. And to say that all we seek is an alliance. Nothing more."

The senior administrator spoke for the first time since their arrival. "Alliance is a slippery term."

"A strong and trusted ally on Aldwyn," Logan replied. "Someone we can trust after we return to Cygneus Prime."

That drew bitter mirth from Linux. "You're leaving us to mop up your mess, is that it?"

The general said, "Havoc is four times our size. Maybe five. They'll come against us in force—"

"We are not leaving," Logan said, "until the issue with Havoc is resolved."

"Then you will die and your bones will be entombed on Aldwyn," Linux sneered. "That is, if Havoc leaves more than dust and regret."

"That is entirely possible." Logan rose from his seat. "I will not keep you any longer."

35

Sean and Dillon were summoned back to the militia captain's office. Logan was seated behind the desk, flanked by his two officers and Sidra. When they entered, he asked, "Have you seen action?"

"We have. Yes." Dillon's response was so fast, Sean had to assume he had been expecting the question.

"I don't mean some mock exercise with other cadets, in the safety of a schoolyard."

"The answer is the same," Dillon said.

Sean said, "Dillon is the soldier. Not me."

Dillon shook his head. "Sean was as involved as anybody in the assault. Maybe more."

Logan seemed pleased by the exchange. "Assault?"

"A planet called Lothia," Dillon said. "We took part in defeating the aliens' last attack."

Vance asked, "Aliens?"

"Later," Logan said.

Sean told his brother, "I did what I needed to do. You fought. There's a difference and you know it."

"Everybody with brains is scared going in," Vance said.

"You did great when it was all on the line," Dillon said. "You saved the day."

Sean told Logan, "I'll do whatever you say. But I'm a diplomat by training and temperament."

Dillon snorted. "You're selling yourself short."

Logan had clearly heard enough. "Say we agree with your plan to hunt inside the Havoc fief. What do you need to make this happen?"

§

What Sean needed was solitude and a bit of peace and quiet. Which he was not going to get. Logan insisted that Sean use a pallet laid out by the side wall. His glare challenged the twins to complain about the audience.

Sean stretched out and shut his eyes. He heard Dillon pull over a chair and position it by the pallet. His brother gripped Sean's left shoulder. Anchoring him to the here and now. Saying more clearly than words ever could that they were a team.

Sean closed his eyes, took a long breath, released it slowly. He pushed everything into his gut, down to the point where the power to transit resided. He fashioned an energy bubble and compacted everything inside—his thoughts and emotions and fears and life. Then he just . . .

Went.

Sean drew up from his physical form and hovered there in

the empty space above the six people gathered in the office—Logan, Dillon, Vance, Nicolette, Sidra, and himself. He saw how Dillon's eyes were clenched tight, like he was trying to consume Sean's confusion and fatigue, and replace them with his own strength. Then Vance spoke softly, and Nicolette shushed him. Sean caught the whiff of emotional tension between them, an old flavor, not good but healing.

He turned away from the people and the room. He directed his attention to the target.

And he flew.

At the end of the Havoc tunnel, Sean passed through three huge chambers. The first contained the vanished market guards and several hundred merchants, all allies of Clan Havoc who had fled Logan's arrival. The housing looked temporary and cramped. Sean passed over people lined up for a soup kitchen–style meal. They did not seem very concerned for a group that had recently been kicked out of their homes, which confirmed what Sean had suspected. The battle was far from over.

The second cavern held a military barracks and parade ground and training area. A large number of soldiers were prepping for the attack on Hawk territory. Sean searched the troops but could sense no strangeness, no secret weapon.

In that instant he caught the first faint whiff of danger.

He could not identify the source. He could not even tell if the peril was directed at him. The presence carried a faint hint of venom, very old, very angry.

Sean waited a long moment, wondering if he should turn back. But the danger did not strengthen. In fact, it seemed to withdraw. Sean's impression was of an evil lighthouse sweeping across some vast distance, passing on.

He pressed on.

Clan Havoc's third cavern was by far the largest Sean had ever seen and contained a fortified empire. Groves of trees ringed a fair-sized town, and beyond that was a castle, with guard towers and banners and courtyards and a massive outer gate. From the cavern's other side stretched a vast array of tunnels that Sean knew led to mines and Tiko's smelting operations.

Inside the palace's main hall, Sean found his prey. Three senior Diplomats. In Duke Tiko's audience hall.

They were led by his enemy. Kaviti.

Just as Sean identified his nemesis, the distant peril swiveled back in his direction. He was certain it did not originate from Clan Havoc. But that did not lessen the sense of threat.

This time, the peril shifted away, only to return and *fasten* upon him. Sean felt like he was suddenly bathed in a superheated lava flow. The volcanic fury was off-world, he was certain of that. The peril shrieked like a thousand band saws. Totally inhuman. Readying for an assault.

Sean zipped back. Gasped. He bolted to his feet, only to fall back to the pallet. He heaved a terrible breath.

Dillon said, "Tell me."

"They're coming."

Logan demanded, "How many?"

"Hard to tell. A lot of them."

Dillon asked, "Did you see the weapon?"

"No. But it's there."

"How do you know?" This from Vance.

Sean looked at his brother. "I saw three senior Diplomats."

Logan asked, "Ghost-walkers from your group? Working with Havoc?"

"Ambassador Kaviti is one of them," Sean said.

His brother actually smiled. "For real?"

"He's leading the crew."

Dillon laughed out loud. "Bro, you just made my day."

36

Sean transited to Cylian's office first. Finding it empty, he shifted to her apartment. A bored-looking young Messenger was sprawled in Cylian's parlor. She leapt to her feet at Sean's appearance and demanded, "You are the agent the Ambassador's team has been awaiting?"

Sean repressed the first response that came to mind, which was, *How many other men have popped into Cylian's private quarters?* He said, "Yes. I'm Sean."

"I've been stationed here with orders to inform her the instant you arrive, Major."

"Tell Cylian I can only stay — " Sean stopped because the young woman was already gone.

Sean could not completely hide his disappointment when both Carver and Anyon showed up with Cylian. The colonel wore a full-dress uniform. Anyon and Cylian were decked out in formal evening attire. They looked utterly exhausted. Strain etched itself as deep as flesh-colored tattoos on all three faces. Cylian looked on the brink of collapse. Sean wanted to demand to know what was going on, offer help, whatever. But there was no time. Logan had loaned Sean his own timepiece, which was now strapped to his left wrist. The amount of time he had been granted here was already half over.

Carver said, "Report."

"The weapons exist," Sean replied. "We have not seen one. But the reports came from a source who did not know we were searching for them."

"Perhaps the source is a plant," Anyon fretted. He still carried a dinner napkin in his left hand.

"Our ally on Aldwyn is named Logan. He and his crew have developed a method of transiting all on their own. He has used this to recapture a market cavern from their foes, Clan Havoc. The information came from one of their troopers." Sean gave that a quick breath, then added, "There's more."

"Speak."

"There are three senior members of the Assembly dealing with Havoc. They supplied the technology to develop these weapons. They insisted on the production remaining on Aldwyn."

Anyon understood instantly. "So it could be kept secret from us."

"That is our thinking," Sean said. "One of the Diplomats is Kaviti."

Anyon sank into a chair. Wiped his forehead with the napkin. "Tell me everything."

Sean gave it to them as quickly as he could. As he was finishing, Logan's timepiece pinged. "I have to leave."

"We need to plan," Anyon protested.

"You'll have to do so without me," Sean replied.

Carver asked, "Can I return with you?"

"Negative. They don't trust us." He shot Cylian a look that he hoped carried some of the emotions he was feeling.

"Wait!" Carver stepped toward him. "What is your assessment?"

"The Assembly was asked to come now because the ruling council on Cygneus Prime heard about Havoc, the Diplomats, and the weapon." The words tumbled out. "You are intended to serve as their shield against this unknown threat."

"What comes next?"

Sean did not have time to soften the news. "War."

37

Logan emerged from his strategy session accompanied by his officers and noncoms. He found Kyle, the corporal guard, waiting in the corridor. "Did the twin return?"

"Twenty seconds late." Kyle handed over the timepiece. "He asks to speak with you."

"Where are they now?"

"Scouting the market area over by the tunnel. Sidra's with them. I hope that's okay, sir. You didn't say nothing about holding them here."

"You did right, Corporal." He signaled for Vance and Nicolette to join him. "Let's move out."

They found the twins standing in the middle of the broad avenue leading to the tunnel's entrance. When they came into view, Logan halted where he and his officers could observe the two off-worlders. He watched Sean and Dillon huddle, their hands shaping structures in the cavern's dusty air.

"They're working on something, sure enough," Vance said.

Logan nodded. "Have they discussed a strategy?"

"Not with me."

Kyle said, "The quiet one, Sean. He said he had half an idea."

"Looks like more than half to me," Vance said.

Logan disliked the feeling this gave him, having his authority challenged in such a way. Their survival rested on a knife's edge. It was unsettling to think that their existence might come down to trusting these two.

The twins chose that moment to break off their conversation and come trotting over.

Sean said, "Dillon has a plan."

"It was your idea," Dillon corrected. "I just put meat on the bones."

"Tell me," Logan said.

Sean did most of the talking. He sketched out a concept that had promise, but only if Logan was willing to place these two off-worlders at the center of their unit.

Logan wished he had a chance to step back and ponder. For days, if need be. His entire life had been built around the secrecy that was only possible when all outsiders were treated as potential foes.

When Sean stopped, Logan decided he had no choice but to accept their plan. His uncle's refusal to offer support had stripped him of the freedom to take an alternate route. It was either this, or die. Of course, they could still retreat. Which was . . .

Logan realized there was something he had to do. Now. Before the battle. While he still could claim a breath as his own. He needed to seek the counsel of a general who understood the risk involved in trusting strangers.

He said to Vance, "I need to report in."

"You mean, talk with Gerrod?" Vance frowned. "I doubt you'll find any help in that quarter. The general's adjutant wants to watch you fail."

"Which is why I intend to go directly to General Brodwyn." He turned to Sidra. "Can you take me back to Cygneus?"

The fierce young woman showed an instant's dismay. "Cross space? With you?"

"You've taken prisoners to Aldwyn's far side. You've jumped from the surface to Hattie's ship. The only difference is the distance you'll be covering."

Vance asked, "You're sure that's necessary?"

"Vital," Logan said. He turned back to Sidra. "Well?"

Before she could respond, Sean said, "I volunteer."

That turned them all around. "You can do this?" Logan asked.

"Indirectly. I'll bring you in contact with the Assembly's representatives. They'll take you where you want to go."

"Can I trust these off-worlders?"

"With your life," Sean replied.

Vance asked, "You've crossed space with others in your care?"

Dillon replied, "Hundreds of times. More."

Logan saw a sudden confluence of forces, a drawing together of multiple strands of fate. He said to Dillon, "Put your plans into action."

The twin showed a warrior's grin. "Immediately."

Logan turned to the others. "Nicolette, Vance, Sidra, you will accompany me?"

It was Nicolette who replied, "To the galaxy's hidden depths."

"Let's hope that won't be necessary." Logan reached out a hand to Sean. "Quick, now. Time is not our ally."

38

ogan's undercurrent of fear heightened as Sean gestured for them to link up. But there was nothing he could do about it. Logan gripped the off-worlder's hand and said, "Go."

Ghost-walking was smoother with Sean than with any of his own people. He mentally spoke the word they used. *Transiting.* The act was as simple as taking a next step. Half a second later, they stood inside a pleasant and spacious dwelling. The chambers Logan could see were empty. "Where are they?"

"A Messenger is supposed to be on constant duty. We shouldn't need to wait long."

"Do you really think I can be trained to travel like this?"

"If you can detect other . . . ghost-walkers, then my guess is, absolutely. But that's not something I know much about. Yet."

"Where are we?"

"Serena. Capital of the Human Assembly."

"How far . . ."

"I don't know exactly. A long, long way." There was the sound of water running. "Heads up. We're on."

A young woman in a sky-blue uniform appeared in the rear corridor. She showed alarm at the sight of them standing in her parlor. "My apologies, Major! So sorry to keep you waiting, sir!"

"No, wait—" Sean began, but the woman was already gone.

Logan asked, "Major?"

Sean looked embarrassed. "Anyone appointed to the Diplomats' school is brevetted major. But it's just to get things done."

"I would imagine some trainees take advantage of the rank," Logan said.

"Probably. I don't know for certain. I've only had the assignment for two days."

Logan turned to Sidra. "It's time for you to check on the situation."

Just as Sidra vanished, a genuine beauty appeared, a flash of brilliance so strong the room paled simply by holding her.

Sean said, "Advocate Cylian, this is—"

A man in an officer's formal uniform appeared, followed by an older gentleman in the finery of high office. The officer had an empty sleeve pinned to his upper arm.

"Ambassador Anyon, Colonel Carver, Advocate Cylian," Sean said. "This is Commander Logan and his two adjutants, Vance and Nicolette."

The Ambassador demanded, "You speak the tongue used by the Cygnean ruling council?"

"Centuries before the council came into existence, it was known as the Hawk tongue," Logan replied. "I speak it."

Sean said, "Logan is heir to the Hawk fief."

"Which no longer exists," Logan added. "I serve the ruling council on Cygneus Prime."

Sean went on, "He needs to speak with his commanding officer, a General Brodwyn."

Cylian said, "She serves as the military's representative to our negotiations."

"She may wish to send her adjutant, Gerrod," Logan said. "Tell her that is not acceptable."

"Time is crucial," Sean said.

"In that case, I should make the request personally." Anyon motioned to Carver. "Colonel, attend me."

When the two men vanished, Sean said, "Something is wrong."

Cylian did indeed look both strained and exhausted. She wiped her face. "We are under great pressure."

"It's more than that," Sean insisted.

"Perhaps this should wait."

"Cylian. This could be important."

"The first two nights, the Ambassador's entire team experienced savage dreams. Now we are sleeping here on Serena."

Sean shook his head like a boxer throwing off sweat. "Anyon wouldn't make a shift like that just because of nightmares. Tell me the rest."

She glanced at the others. "Anyon's Watchers started their first planetary survey, then . . ."

Logan asked, "Watchers?"

"She means those transiters, ghost-walkers, who have heightened their senses. They do what I did, the hunt. And they do what you do, searching out new transiters." Sean turned back to the woman. "Tell me what happened, Cylian."

"One came back screaming. He's been sedated ever since. The other . . . She won't wake up."

"What—" Sean's next question was cut off by the Ambassador and colonel reappearing. With them was a tall, severe woman with the expression of one who never smiled.

Vance said, "Ten-hut."

39

Sean and the others returned to Aldwyn with another five dozen Cygnean troops. Cylian, Anyon, Carver, Dillon, and Sidra all helped with the transit. Brodwyn herself came over to survey Logan's preparations. If the general was disconcerted by being shifted between planets in the space of half a heartbeat, she gave no sign. She flatly rejected Anyon's request that Praetorian Guards be permitted to enter the conflict. The political implications, she insisted, would make this a council decision, and they did not have either the evidence or the time for such.

They ordered Logan to outline his strategy, and he drew Sean and Dillon into the mix. The general and Anyon both heard them out in silence. When they were done, and all Sean could see was the potential for deadly mistakes, Carver drew the twins aside and said, "You both have the makings of great leaders."

Dillon's only response was to go crimson from his collar to his hairline. Sean said, "Right now I'm filled with the prospect of total failure."

"This, too, is part of leadership. But your plan is a good one." Carver started to turn away, then said, "It is an honor to serve with you." He drew himself up to rigid attention and threw them both a parade-ground salute.

When he had departed, Dillon said, "Talk about making my day."

Sean pointed over to where the general was talking with Logan. "Not just us."

They were too far away to hear what the general was telling Logan. But her words were clearly impacting him very deeply. She noticed them watching and said, "Join us."

Up close, Sean thought Logan had never looked more the leader.

Brodwyn said, "I am making a battlefield promotion of Major Logan, subject to final approval once this sortie is concluded. I take it you have no objection."

"None whatsoever," Sean replied.

"It's a great step," Dillon said. "He deserves it."

"You will be the youngest officer of this rank in Cygnean history," Brodwyn said, and revealed her version of a smile, all taut edges and honed precision. "Keep this up and I will soon be saluting you."

Logan said weakly, "Thank you, General."

She seemed not to notice Logan's struggle for control and waved over her adjutant. Sean's first impression was that Gerrod was a snotty, conceited officer who liked using the general's clout as though it belonged to him personally.

Clearly Sean's opinion was shared by Logan and his officers. Which might have been why the general made such a public display of saying, "I am hereby assigning Gerrod duty as Logan's adjutant."

Gerrod jerked as though he'd been zapped. "General—"

"You may thank me later," she snapped. When she was certain his protest had been stifled, she continued in an even louder voice, "Unless Major Logan directs otherwise, you will be responsible for the newly arrived Cygnean troops. Major Logan's end-of-battle report will have a direct and lasting impact on your own opportunities for advancement. Is that clear?"

Gerrod wilted to the point that Sean almost felt sorry for him. "Perfectly, General."

"Excellent." Brodwyn turned to where the troopers were rendered utterly dumbfounded by the shock of being transited to Aldwyn. "Major?"

Logan nodded to Vance, who shouted, "Attention!"

Brodwyn's voice was made to carry far. "Obey Major Logan as you would me. Learn from the experience. I am certain his tactics will soon be adopted as a major component of our army's battle strategy. Good hunting." She saluted the room, then turned to Anyon and said, "Ambassador?"

When the pair had departed, Logan stepped in close to the twins and said, "I'm very glad indeed that I trusted you."

While they were still absorbing that, Logan turned to his three officers and ordered half of the newly arrived troops to serve as backup to his own crew, and the other to patrol the market. He charged Nicolette and Gerrod with the patrols and sent two of his ghost-walkers with them. There was no telling, he warned, whether Havoc might try to outflank them by transiting in troops of their own. But Sean didn't think that would happen, and Dillon shared his opinion. Senior Diplomats like Kaviti would consider it an insult to transit local troops under orders from an outpost world's duke.

Dillon pulled Sean aside and said, "Want to see what I did on my summer vacation?"

"Absolutely."

Dillon held out his hand. "Grab hold."

They stepped together and wound up on top of a hill that should not have been there.

Sean took a slow look around. "You've been busy."

While he was away, Sean's plan had been turned into a dusty fortress. He had figured the Havoc crew assumed they held the element of a double surprise. They possessed a secret weapon, and they were allied to the off-world ghost-walkers. Not to mention the size of the Havoc army.

Odds were overwhelmingly in their favor. The Havoc crew probably assumed they would waltz in and take over.

Sean hoped it might be possible to shock Tiko's forces into the Aldwyn equivalent of next week.

With the help of Logan's team, Dillon had cleared away the first three rows of market stalls fronting the Havoc tunnel. Actually, the local crew had mostly watched, at least at first. Dillon had used the hill's construction as a means of both testing and training Logan's crew. They had showed an uncommon ability to lift and grind and transport. By the time the conical hill was completed, Logan's ghost-walkers had honed a new tactic.

Sean now found the tunnel mouth facing a semicircle of utterly bare stone. The open space extended back about two hundred feet. And it was now rimmed by a semicircular hill. Dillon had fashioned a killing ground.

40

Their rooftop aerie offered a clear view of the entire free-fire zone. The empty space surrounding the tunnel opening was a full one hundred paces wide. The semicircular hill was fifteen paces high and gently sloped. A flat space had been pounded along its top to form a guard's walk. Twenty-five troops in militia uniforms knelt on the opposite side, their shoulders and weapons partly visible from the tunnel mouth. Kneeling there in silent warning.

Every time he glanced over the rooftop wall and surveyed the perimeter defenses and the paltry number of troops on guard, Sean's gut crawled with fear. He tasted their vulnerability and all the unanswered questions with every breath. Doom had never felt closer.

Dillon handled the waiting with irritating ease. Unlike his brother, for whom every sound carried the threat of an invading force. Finally Sean demanded, "How can you stay so calm?"

Dillon was stretched out on a pallet with his back against the wall supporting the interior stairwell, his eyes half closed. He pointed with his chin toward the faces peering over the militia headquarters' rooftop, which towered above every other structure in the market. "The scouts will see any movement. Your job is to chill."

Sean threw himself down beside his brother. They were stationed on the roof of the second highest structure, which had been fashioned into an outdoor living area. "I hate this waiting."

Dillon stretched out his legs. "You ever wonder where we'd be if, you know, none of this had happened? Transit, Academy, aliens, worlds, all that."

"No. You?"

"Lately. Yeah. Some." Dillon gave that a long beat, then confessed, "I wonder if Carey and I could have made a go of it."

"You'd give this up for her?"

"I thought about it. For about five minutes."

"You mean, what life would have been like if we'd never known this existed." Sean was tracking with his brother now. "If you had them wipe your memory. Like that."

Dillon did not respond.

This was a less-than-ideal moment to go all personal with his brother. But Sean wanted it said. Just in case. "I need to tell you something. About Carey."

"Go on, then."

"You were right to break it off."

There was no change that anybody else would have noticed. But Sean knew his brother, and he could see how much it cost Dillon to keep the mask in place.

"In case you missed the point," Dillon replied, "Carey was the one who did all the breakage."

"She might have wielded the hammer. But you knew what was coming down." Sean gave him a chance to object, then went on, "And you let it happen. Because you knew it was the right move."

Dillon's gaze swiveled back to the empty space rimming the tunnel. "If only."

"You knew then, you know now," Sean insisted. "Carey loved the guy you were. Not the man you're becoming."

Dillon clenched his jaw so tight the muscles in his neck stood out. He did not reply.

"You know who you want to be," Sean said. "It's your basic nature. You've been aiming for this all your life."

Dillon's voice sounded strangled. "Carey blames it all on transiting."

"It gave you the chance to spread your wings, sure. But this is who you are."

Dillon was quiet. Finally he said, "She told me I was too busy killing the best part of me to save us."

Sean winced with the shared pain. "Dillon, you're becoming the man you were meant to be. Either she loves this facet of you—"

"She doesn't. She won't."

"Then hard as it is," Sean said, "you did the right thing. At the right time. Before your relationship went any further."

Dillon responded with a move from their earliest days,

ducking his head and hiding behind hair that had been lost to his military crew cut.

His struggle for control was enough to push Sean to speak words he had been thinking about for almost a year. Only now he wished he had spoken them a lot earlier. "I'm really proud of you."

41

Two seconds later, everything shifted from tense boredom and secret discussions to bedlam. And it all started with a whistle.

Sean rose with his brother and saw Vance personally flashing the signal from the headquarters' rooftop.

"Showtime," Dillon said. "Finally."

Sean started to tell Dillon exactly how much he was not looking forward to this, when he heard shouts and running feet from inside the tunnel.

The Havoc troops invaded in force. Two officers in glittering uniforms stepped out and flanked either side of the tunnel as hundreds of soldiers raced forward. Even from this distance, Sean could see their disdain for the hill and the paltry number of militia kneeling behind it.

Dillon muttered, "Looks like they brought a full brigade."

The officers rapped out orders in a language Sean did not understand, but the effect was clear enough. The front positions were given over to shoulder-mounted weapons that looked like miniature cannons, except the nozzles ended in polished cones.

"Blasters of some sort," Dillon said.

The officers stepped closer together and talked tactics as the ground forces formed two tight lines, the front kneeling, the second row standing. They took aim.

One of the officers then shouted in the language Sean understood, "Surrender or die!"

Dillon scooted down and pulled Sean back from the wall. "Not the most original warning I've ever heard."

Two officers shouted something else. And the cavern was rocked by incoming fire.

Which was exactly what they had hoped would happen.

Ruse within a ruse.

The plan had never been about defending the hill. The intent was to force the Havoc troops to reveal their hand. Which they did in spectacular fashion.

The top of the hill erupted into a massive cloud of dust and debris. Each round gouged a deep crevice in Dillon's creation. Sean had been worried about Havoc troops shooting holes in the cavern roof, but clearly these soldiers were well accustomed to the danger of death by vacuum, and aimed low. Which made the damage they wreaked on the hill even more severe.

But none of it mattered. At least, not to Logan's troops.

Because they were all gone.

Two of the militia had been assigned to each of Logan's ghost-walkers. As soon as the first Havoc command was yelled, they dropped down and grabbed hold of the nearest ghost-walker, and together they all took a giant step back.

Before the first shot blasted the hill, they were all safely on the rooftops that made up their secondary positions. A distant rim of protection, well removed from the line of fire.

Sean's view of the Havoc tunnel was lost to the blanket of dust and debris. His forward vision was limited to glimpses of the obliterated hill. Dillon's perimeter defense was reduced now by half.

Just as they had wanted.

From somewhere beyond Sean's field of vision, there came another shouted command. The attack halted. The silence was deafening. Sean could see very little, the dust was so thick.

One of Logan's crew moaned loudly. Which was part of their ruse. Another cried he was hit. When a third wailed in helpless terror, several of the attackers laughed.

Dillon said softly, "So far so good."

* * *

Sean's second foray into conflict was different from the first in every way imaginable.

The first time, he had been fighting aliens. He had known what to do because he had been granted a single brief glimpse into the cloud of knowing—a sort of bodiless library set in place by an unknown group called the Ancients.

This time, he had to figure things out for himself.

All his planning had one goal. To avoid costing lives. On both sides.

The comm link Logan had supplied them was a black band attached to Sean's left wrist with a strap that slipped around his thumb. The strap had five buttons, intended to grant the wearer five different channels through which to communicate. All five of Sean's connected him to Logan's team.

Sean pressed the only button that worked, and the earpiece responded with Vance saying, "Go."

"Time to start round two."

"Thirty seconds," Vance confirmed, and clicked off.

The Havoc officers shouted something that Sean assumed was their version of "Charge!" Their troops raced across the empty stone floor—or tried to. But nothing could have prepared them for the pounding that commenced.

Shield and attack. Shield and attack. The challenge had formed the third and most boring lesson in Sean and Dillon's early training. Of course, that particular exercise had taken place in the safety of their backyard. This was something else entirely.

Dillon's work on the hill had resulted in all of the local transiters strengthening those same two abilities. From the safety of their rear positions, Logan's ghost-walkers hefted the hill's rubble and flung it at the Havoc invaders.

The lieutenant stood his ground and ordered his troopers to form lines and take aim. Which was when Dillon started adding his own signature to the tempest. But it was not in the form of more rocks, as Sean had expected. Instead, he started making little finger motions, tight gestures that matched his focused expression. Gradually the billowing dust condensed until it formed a single impenetrable mass.

Dillon then directed the cloud down onto the Havoc troops. It choked off any hope they had of breathing.

The Havoc troops had no choice but to retreat back into their tunnel.

The stone plaza was empty now. The tunnel opening was being pelted by stones and blocks of cement and bits of wood. The only sound was the yells of victory from Logan's troops.

Dillon turned to Sean and said, "Time for round three."

The plan was for Sean to transit with Logan and his officers to the palace forecourt. Dillon would stay with them only so long as was required to find a niche from which he might serve as backup. Then Logan would offer Tiko the chance to surrender.

No one expected Tiko to fold. The aim was to show that Havoc was vulnerable to attack from within. That it was in their best interest to withdraw and make peace. A lasting arrangement between two sworn enemies, was how Dillon put it. Sometimes that was the best that could be hoped for.

In the meantime, Sean intended to ask Tiko to pass on a message to Kaviti—that he and Dillon were there under orders from the Human Assembly. Kaviti was hereby commanded to give himself up. Then the twins Kaviti had falsely arrested would happily escort him back to Serena and stick him in the same cage where he had tried to trap them. Let Kaviti experience *real* Assembly justice. From the receiving end.

Of course, Kaviti would have already scampered away by that point. All Sean needed to do was speak the guy's name and Kaviti would be off to some shadowy corner of a forgotten outpost world, where he'd spend the rest of his life fearing the next knock on the door. The message was for Tiko's benefit. Let him know the game was up.

Once Tiko realized his off-world team had scampered, Sean figured the duke would fold like a bad tent.

※※※

Their arrival on the militia headquarters' rooftop was greeted by utter silence, which Sean took as a very good sign. Logan surveyed the rubble-strewn space between them and the tunnel. Gerrod stood beside him, rendered silent by the shock of what he had just witnessed.

Sean said, "It's time."

Logan yelled, "Cease firing!"

Vance passed the order through his comm link. Hundreds of rocks plunked heavily down to earth. A few yells resonated through the empty air, then silence. The dust drifted slowly to earth. From somewhere far down the tunnel emerged the faint sounds of hacking coughs and cries and running feet.

Sean reached for his brother and asked, "Ready?"

Logan walked over and gripped Sean's other arm. "Nicolette, you are in command. Sidra, Vance, Gerrod, join us."

The general's adjutant was clearly terrified of enduring another transit. It required several seconds and sheer force of will for Gerrod to reach over and grip Vance's arm.

Sean said, "Step with me. On three. One, two . . ."

That was the moment everything fell apart.

42

The lone attacker was dressed exactly as their turncoat had described. Sean thought it looked like a track suit, hood and all. The grey material was a shade or two lighter than slate and revealed a very fine grey mesh that glinted as he moved. The blade he carried was the exact same color. The weapon was far too long to be called a knife. It was a more like a short sword, rapier thin and curved slightly. The blade and the man's clothing seemed to absorb all light, as though man and blade together formed an implement that was meant to suck out their prey's life.

And he was *fast*.

They were all taken aback by his speed. Dillon was the only one who managed to get off a blast of his own. But it did no good. There was still enough dust in the air for Sean to see the vibrations as Dillon's assault split and flowed to either side of the assailant, leaving him untouched.

The attacker stepped forward and flicked out his blade. It was an almost casual gesture, except that it was blindingly swift. His target was Logan.

Sean instinctively shot out a shield. Nicolette shrieked and drew her sidearm, as did Vance and Gerrod. The blade was faster.

But Sidra was swifter still.

The street waif revealed both lightning reflexes and a tiger's strength. She leapt in front of Logan and shoved him so hard he fell over backward, landing hard enough to punch out his breath.

The blade sank into Sidra's back. Right at heart level.

She crumpled to the stones without a sound.

This time Nicolette's shriek was joined by a multitude of other yells, including Sean's. Four weapons fired on the Assassin—Nicolette's and Vance's and Kyle's and Gerrod's. Sean blasted him with the transiter's force, as did Dillon. Two fists of helpless rage.

Only he was no longer there.

"No!" Kyle crumpled to the stones beside Sidra. He cradled the tiny inert form, stroked her face, rocked back and forth. "No!"

Logan's face was terrible to behold. He gripped one of Sidra's limp hands and stared at the young-old face. Silent. Immobile. He let Kyle wail for him.

"Sean." Dillon's expression was unlike anything Sean had ever seen before. His brother showed Logan a warrior's fierce intent. "We need to strike."

"Wait," Sean said. He looked down at a shattered Logan. Sean knew he was going to have to step up and think for them all in that moment. But that was okay.

Dillon growled, "Sean . . ."

"I said *wait*."

His tone not only silenced his brother, it also drew the attention of everyone except Kyle. Even Logan glanced over. Sean told them, "We all know this changes everything."

Dillon said, "The gloves come off."

"We have a window," Sean said. His voice was astonishingly calm. His heart was hammering, his mind was racing, his fury was a volcanic rush. But his voice revealed none of this. He kept his gaze on Logan, giving the commander his due. "They think we'll be in total confusion from what we've just seen."

"Our defenses have been torn wide open," Dillon said. "They have ghost-walkers. They have weapons we shouldn't know anything about. They'll be preparing an attack. On their schedule. When they're good and ready. The clock is theirs to control."

"But they're wrong," Sean said. "If we act fast."

It was Nicolette who said, "Tell us what you're thinking."

Sean laid out his idea as swiftly as he could manage, knowing he left more gaps than solutions. Then he waited.

Vance walked over and touched a dark spot on the wall. He inspected his fingers, then held them up to the others. "Blood. We injured their attacker."

"They have others," Gerrod fretted. "And we don't know how many."

"They won't matter," Dillon said. "As soon as their off-world superiors realize we know who they are and what they're up to, they'll freak."

"But we have to act fast," Sean said.

Logan rose slowly to his feet. The events had aged him a thousand years. "We'll be ready for your signal."

43

Sean transited with Dillon to the far side of the first Havoc cavern, away from the guards stationed by the Hawk tunnel mouth. He scouted quickly, then pointed to an empty ledge two-thirds of the way up the wall. "How about up there?"

"Perfect," Dillon said.

Once they had transited up, Sean told his brother, "Fast as you can."

Dillon shot him a grin that was frightening in its intensity. "Shock and awe."

"Absolutely."

They were no longer after defense.

They wanted obliteration.

Dillon waved his arms like a demented conductor, drawing together a roaring tempest of stone and dust and debris. Faint screams and cries began rising from the cavern floor. Dillon took everything that wasn't living, nailed down or not. He wanted it all.

"Block them from getting anywhere near the tunnel mouth!" Dillon shouted.

"On it." Sean fashioned a shield shaped pretty much like the hill they had just left behind. A curved structure that barred the hysterical mob from approaching Dillon's target. The running, screaming people rammed into the invisible wall and bounced off like a pinball machine gone berserk.

The gun placements stationed by the Hawk tunnel rose off their stanchions and melded into Dillon's tornado. Next came virtually all the buildings, the tents, the kitchen areas, the works. Sean made a mental note to ask Dillon how he managed to avoid sweeping up the people and animals as well. But for the moment he was content to observe his brother grind the cavern's contents in midair.

Dillon hurled the massive shrieking tornado straight into the tunnel mouth.

44

The whirlwind vanished down the connecting tunnel, roaring and shrieking and shaking the ground like a caged beast hungry for release. Dillon kept his arms outstretched and his eyes scrunched shut, then as the sound eased he said, "That's as far as I can push it."

"Let's hope it's far enough." Sean reached for his brother's hand.

They stepped and transited from the first Havoc cavern to the second. And found themselves at the border of a full-fledged panic.

Sean spotted an empty ledge, pointed, and had to shout to be heard. "Up there, two o'clock!"

"Go!"

Once they arrived, the height diminished the clamor to the point that they could hear themselves think. The middle cavern, the one formerly holding the Havoc military compound, was a chaotic mess. The precise layout was gone, replaced by a jumble of men and equipment and debris. Sean could see how Dillon's tornado had roared from the tunnel mouth and sprayed destruction almost the entire way across the vast cavern.

"Time for me to help the others get started," Sean said.

Dillon was already into his windup. "I'm good here."

As Sean started to depart, he had an idea. "Maybe you should seal the mouth leading to Tiko's main cavern."

Dillon hesitated. "Say again?"

"Stop the army here from coming to Tiko's aid. You know, once we move on."

Dillon spared time for a fierce grin. "Go get the others and hurry back. I miss hearing the sound of your brain at work."

***

When Sean returned to the Hawk market cavern, he found Logan and most of his team standing in rough formation in the empty plaza fronting the tunnel mouth. Vance and Nicolette were shaping the teams, squaring them away, prepping for the next step. As per Sean's plan, Gerrod had been sent ahead with a few of the transiters and most of the newly arrived militia. Their aim was to take control of the first Havoc cavern while confusion still reigned.

Logan stood alone, wrapped in a solemn cloak of grimness and loss.

Sean stepped in close. "I'm so sorry."

"Sidra was my first discovery," Logan said, his voice as bleak as his expression. "Sometimes it felt as though I learned my secret craft so I could release her from her chains."

Sean gave that a beat, then said, "Dillon and I are after a certain kind of tactic." As he spoke, Nicolette and Vance drifted into listening range. Sean gave Logan a chance to object, but when their commander remained silent he went on. "It's called stressing the situation. The aim is to keep your opponent off balance. Show him that his assumption of control is all wrong."

"Stressing," Nicolette repeated. "I am liking this word very much."

"The thing is," Sean said, "we have to move fast. There isn't time for . . ."

Logan nodded his understanding.

"We will mourn with you," Vance said, gripping Logan's arm. "Once we have found the man who did this and ground him into the dust."

Logan focused for the first time since Sidra had dropped to the stones. "It's good to rely on the strength of friends."

"That's the word for this hour," Nicolette said. "Friends."

Sean loved having a reason to grin. "Let's go shock Duke Tiko right out of his boots."

45

They arrived in time to watch Dillon's final sweep. At first glance, it appeared that the entire Havoc military machine was now piled up against the tunnel mouth that before had led to the palace hold. The twisted metal and machines and weapons and barracks and supplies formed a multicolored mountain. Up by the cavern's distant ceiling rose an empty, broken flagpole.

Sean pointed and said, "Your work?"

"I thought it made a nice sort of statement." Dillon turned to the others and said, "You might want to step back from the edge. Somebody down there is bound to still have a sidearm."

Sean had his doubts. And even if a Havoc soldier was armed, he doubted they would be able to use it. The impact of Dillon's force had been total. Far below, people milled about with the frantic mindlessness of ants that had just lost their hill. Many appeared to be wearing only fragments of their original uniforms.

Logan demanded, "How do you manage this?"

"Praetorian training is centered on one theme. Maximum impact with minimum loss of life."

Sean pretended not to notice Logan's pain. "Time to move." As the others linked up, he added, "I think maybe we should bring in our superiors. But only if you agree."

Logan glanced at his officers.

"I agree," Vance said.

Nicolette nodded. "Brodwyn needs to see this."

"Very well." He said to Sean, "Make it happen."

Sean started to say that Logan needed to come and make the request official, but a fractional head shake from Nicolette kept the words unspoken.

"In the meantime, we will continue stressing the Havocs," Nicolette said.

"Now you're singing my tune," Dillon said.

46

The same young woman was there in Cylian's parlor. Only this time when Sean arrived she saluted and declared, "The Advocate is resting in the back room, Major."

Sean's question was cut off by a faint cry emanating down the hallway. He told the ensign, "I need to speak with Brodwyn, Anyon, and Carver. On the double."

"Right away, sir!" She vanished.

As he rushed down the hall, a weak voice cried, "Sean?"

"Coming!"

When he entered the bedroom, Cylian collapsed back onto her pillow. "I was so worried!"

"What's going on?"

"I've been . . ." Her eyes drifted downward. She fought against it and lost. "I can't . . . Oh."

Sean stroked her face and called her name, then realized a third person in white stood by the side wall. He recognized

Sandrine, now serving as medical officer to the Watchers' Academy. "What happened to her?"

"We know very little for certain." She kept her gaze on the silent form as she said, "Last night's banquet went on until very late. Afterward they returned to Serena, as had become the habit since the Watchers . . . This morning they returned to Cygneus Prime. It appears that Cylian dozed off in a meeting. She woke up screaming from a nightmare that would not release her. She's been like this all day."

Sean turned at the sound of people rushing down the adjoining hallway. Anyon and Carver and Brodwyn crowded into the bedroom. The two Assembly officials looked scarcely better than Cylian, their faces creased with exhaustion and very real pain.

Sean asked Sandrine, "Has she said anything?"

"A few words, in a tongue no one understands," Sandrine replied. "If it is speech at all."

Anyon demanded, "Does Clan Havoc have access to weapons of this sort?"

"No," Sean replied, touching Cylian's cheek, willing her to wake up. "Not a chance."

"How can you be so certain?"

"Their leader, Duke Tiko, is terrified of transiters and everything they represent. He's working with Kaviti only because that group's aims are off-world." Sean gripped the limp hand and turned to the others. "Could someone or something attached to the Human Assembly have done this?"

"Not possible." Carver was absolutely firm. "This breaks the core component of our Praetorian code."

Sean had suspected as much. But he had to be certain. He turned back to Sandrine. "Can you record everything she says?"

"Of course, if you think . . ."

"It could be important. Vital."

"I will set it up immediately."

"Also, next time she awakens, ask her if there was a lighthouse in her nightmare."

"I'm sorry, a what?"

"A beacon. One with a death ray that sweeps in a circle."

Sandrine turned pale. "That is exactly what the surviving Watcher has described."

Anyon demanded, "What does it mean?"

"Not the aliens again," Carver said. "It's too soon."

Reluctantly Sean rose to his feet. He thought he knew the answer, but it had to wait. "We need to go. In the meantime, have the duty ensign pull all Assembly reps off Cygneus Prime."

Anyon protested, "Our negotiations with their ruling council have reached a critical stage."

"They are to transit off and not return," Sean insisted, forcing himself to turn from the lovely young woman. "Do it or face more casualties."

"But—"

Sean's patience broke wide open. "We don't have time for this! For once in your life, try following a directive without wasting everybody's time!"

What Carver and Brodwyn thought of the most senior representative of the Human Assembly being barked at by the most junior was covered by discreet coughs.

Anyon's face turned beet red, but he merely nodded and turned to the wide-eyed ensign. "Do as he says."

"Aye, sir." She glanced at Sean, then vanished.

Sean reached out both hands and said, "We're headed for Tiko's main hold."

47

The first thing that struck Sean upon their arrival back in the Havoc central cavern was the perfumed air.

He should have expected it. He had noticed the grove of trees when he passed through, hunting. Dillon stood behind a line of shrubbery that hid him from the palace ramparts. The trees formed a living barrier between the shrubs and the town fronting the central keep. A stream ran between the trees and the village. Sean had to assume it was driven by underground pumps. The sight was as ostentatious a display of wealth as the grove. Most of the trees were blooming varieties, and many branches were heavy with fruit. The fragrance was jarring. Sean noticed the dry, acrid smell of the lifeless caverns most intensely now.

Logan, Dillon, and the officers had split their troops into three groups. Half of the local transiters were spread in a semicircle with Logan and Dillon at its center. Their aim was to gather ammo in the form of rocks and hardware, and maintain high alert. Any newcomer who popped into view, grey suited or not, was to be annihilated.

Nicolette stepped over, saluted Brodwyn, and told Sean, "My teams are ready and all have the same order. Protect your brother at all costs."

Vance's group was stationed farther away, sheltered behind an outcrop from the cavern wall. The stone walls were ornately carved and rimmed by mock pillars. When Brodwyn asked what they were, Logan replied, "The Havoc crest forms the centerpiece of each side. The chamber probably serves as a family shrine."

Vance's team was already busy taking rocks and earth and small shrubs and flinging them at the palace. Most of their energy was directed at the parapets and town's guard towers. Massive holes along the castle's outer wall suggested former gun placements that had been obliterated.

Vance stepped over to the officers, his grin making a mockery of his salute. "We haven't seen a head, much less a weapon, in far too long."

Gerrod's troops were arrayed in skirmish teams surrounding both groups of transiters. They kept up a constant barrage of small-arms fire at the palace ramparts and the town's guard towers.

Brodwyn stared up at the vast yellow-stone edifice. "Tiko's forebears were the most brutal of the Cygnean pirates. They smuggled, they pillaged, they used the Outer Rim as their base."

Gerrod said, "They still teach the battle tactics used to defeat the Havoc pirate fleet at officer's academy."

Logan stared at the palace with bleak intent and did not speak.

"They've got a lot to answer for," Brodwyn said. She laid a hand on Logan's shoulder and said, "Sean tells me you have suffered a great loss."

He seemed to maintain control only with great effort. "She was my first and closest friend."

"There is nothing that can be said to fill the empty void caused by losing a friend in battle," Brodwyn said. "But enduring this is part of being a true leader. Do you understand what I'm saying?"

Logan did not respond.

"I find it necessary, tragic as it may sound, to observe this trait in my subordinates before appointing them to high command." Her hand lifted once and settled back. "It is an honor to serve with you."

Logan managed, "Thank you, General."

Sean gave that a moment, then said to Dillon, "Time for phase two."

Carver stepped up to Dillon and said, "May I offer my support?"

"Absolutely." Dillon revealed a warrior's grin. "Let's go wake the guy up."

48

As the two Praetorians started their windup, Sean stepped over to Anyon and said, "I owe you an apology."

The Ambassador kept his stern visage aimed at Dillon and Carver and their growing tempests. "Do you?"

"I didn't need to talk to you like that. And I sure didn't need to do it in public."

The two tornadoes sucked up debris and shrubs and rocks and outlying structures. When Dillon plucked up the entire stone shrine, all of Logan's crew cheered.

Anyon surveyed the impact Carver's whirlwind was having on the empty market stalls bordering the town. "I appreciate your apology. But upon reflection, I think your comments and tone were both well deserved."

Sean had no idea how to respond.

Anyon turned to face him. "For any slight and slur, every wrong assumption and dark thought, every mistake I have made regarding you and your brother, I apologize."

"Ambassador, sir, I . . ." Sean decided the only words that really fit were, "Thank you."

Anyon offered a Diplomat's smile—a hint of warmth, a brief easing of the lines of care and concern. Then he said, "Perhaps now would be a good time to consider our options once this so-called duke surrenders."

* * *

When the whirlwinds reached their zenith, Dillon yelled at Carver, "You cover the parapets. I'll knock on Tiko's door."

Carver's only response was to make a grand windmill motion with his arm. As he did so, the funnel turned on its side and began a slow and gradual demolition of the castle's fortifications. The faint sound of screams and clanging bells sounded from unseen courtyards. Carver's tempest moved steadily from left to right, giving the castle a Praetorian haircut.

As Dillon tightened his funnel into a writhing, greyish-yellow battering ram, one of Logan's crew screamed, "Grey Blade! Grey Blade!"

The attacker did not stand a chance.

A hundred rocks struck him at once. A thousand. The ditrinium suit might have protected him against transit force. He also must have had some sort of portable shield of his own.

But he had no protection against the mountain that fell on top of him. And just kept building.

Sean had space for one thought, wondering how the man could transit from inside that suit. Then Dillon shifted the funnel over sideways and yelled, "Knock knock!" He flung his whirlwind at the palace's main portals. The entire funnel disappeared into the palace.

Carver dropped his arms, allowing his own tempest to fade into a torrent of rocks and dust.

Sean only noticed the tornadoes' clamor now, when it was reduced to a muted growl. They could hear more shouts and wails from inside the palace, punctuated by several great crashes.

Every window in the palace blew outward. The three towers that had been sliced open by Carver's tempest shot out great spumes of dust. The one still-intact tower blew its top.

Carver said, "I think they've probably had enough."

Dillon lowered his arms. The clattering rumble faded away. The silence was overwhelming.

Anyon turned to Brodwyn and said, "General, perhaps you should lead the way."

49

errod and the Cygnean militia entered the castle forecourts in force, supported by half of Logan's crew. Sean waited with the senior officers. General Brodwyn and Anyon both agreed that their approach to the palace must take place according to the time-bound protocol of victors.

As they waited for the all clear, Sean was struck by a sudden realization. The shock was electric.

Dillon saw the change and demanded, "What's the matter?"

Sean waved him away, desperate to keep weaving the tendrils of realization together into a cohesive form.

Dillon laughed softly. "Everybody else is getting ready to celebrate. But my brother's already moved on to the next crisis."

The problem was, Dillon was right. Everything Sean had been experiencing on the periphery became the center of it all.

Their imprisonment, the trial, Kaviti and his secret cadre,

the Grey Blades, Logan and his team, even this assault on Tiko's stronghold—all of it faded into the background.

Anyon must have heard Dillon's comments, for he stepped closer and demanded, "What is it?"

Sean's mouth opened and shut twice. He could see it all coalescing. But he wasn't there yet.

Anyon, however, was not made for patience. "Can we proceed?"

Carver found the exchange important enough to translate for the locals. The fact that the senior representative of the Human Assembly had just asked permission from his most junior aide was not lost on anyone. They waited together until Sean finally spoke.

"There's a problem. A big one. But it's not here."

"Connected to this current situation?"

On this point, Sean was definite. "Absolutely."

"Are we safe?"

"For the moment." Sean hated being the one to dilute the moment of triumph with more worries. Yet he had no choice. "But not for long."

* * *

As soon as Gerrod sent word that the area was secure, they entered the palace forecourt with Logan's remaining crew on full alert. Dillon and Carver led the way. The Cygnean militia stood sentry over a multitude of palace guards and courtiers, all of whom looked utterly wasted by the assault. They were filthy, their features slack with shock, their fancy palace uniforms in utter ruin. As was the palace itself. Huge cracks ran up the front walls. The entire doorway and surrounding stonework were just *gone.*

Anyon said to Carver, "Check the prisoners for any of our own."

Carver said, "They would already have transited."

"No doubt. But we must be certain."

They passed through the vanished portal and entered the demolished main hall. A trio of Gerrod's force stood guard around a terrified dignitary. One of the soldiers saluted Brodwyn and said, "This one claims to be Tiko's senior aide."

The man's uniform was a shambles of torn lace and missing buttons. His hair formed a rat's nest around his filthy face. He cried in a tense falsetto, "What is the meaning of this unlawful incursion into Duke Tiko's—"

General Brodwyn carried such authority that a simple lifting of her hand silenced the man. She demanded, "Do you have authority to speak for your duke?"

"I, er, that is . . ."

"It's a simple enough question. Do you or do you not serve as your leader's official spokesperson?"

"Yes, that is, within reason, but—"

"I am General Brodwyn, military representative of the Cygnean ruling council. I am here to discuss terms of the duke's surrender."

"What? No, that's not—"

"And this gentleman is Ambassador Anyon, senior Diplomat with the Human Assembly. He is here to arrest the off-worlder known as Kaviti, and all of his entourage."

"Except the Grey Blade that murdered my staffer," Logan growled.

"Indeed. That one shall stand trial here." Brodwyn surveyed the ruined castle with evident satisfaction. "If we have his full and unqualified assistance in these matters, Tiko will be permitted to maintain control of one reduced segment of his fief. But only if he aids us now without hesitation and swears allegiance to the ruling council on Cygneus Prime. His first order must be for all remaining troops under his command to lay down their arms."

Anyon added, "He must also agree to give testimony against Kaviti and the other off-worlders before the Human Assembly's high court."

Brodwyn nodded. "You will inform your duke that these terms are not negotiable."

50

uke Tiko was a rotund little man who wore polished boots with three-inch heels. His tiny chin was accented by a pointy beard dyed a ridiculous brown. He emerged reluctantly, then tried for pompous disdain until Brodwyn threatened him with imprisonment in the Serenese jail. The prospect of forced transit to Serena clearly terrified him more than prison. He wilted into plump submission. Even so, loss of his empire came with difficulty. Each point was agreed to with the genuine pain of another tooth pulled.

The longer the negotiations continued, the more each passing second ticked loud as cannon fire. Finally Sean could stand it no longer. He stepped up to where Carver, Dillon, and Anyon observed Brodwyn's determined stance and said, "We need to be going."

For once, Anyon showed no disapproval. "Are you certain time is so critical?"

"I'm not sure of anything. And that's the problem." Sean sighed. "I just have a strong feeling. Nothing more."

Dillon declared, "My brother doesn't *need* anything more."

"As illogical as it sounds," Carver said, "history suggests we should heed his warning."

Logan and Vance stepped away from Brodwyn and demanded a translation. When Carver had explained, Logan asked Sean, "Is this another of your unfinished ideas?"

"Maybe." Sean worked the air with frantic hands. "I wish I could be more certain . . ."

Dillon said, "Stop worrying about being wrong and just tell us."

"I think I know what happened to Cylian and the Assembly's Watchers."

Brodwyn broke off from Tiko's latest unfinished protest and demanded, "What is it?" When Carver repeated his explanation, she said, "Surely this can wait until our current demands are met."

Logan said, "If this one thinks it is urgent, General, I respectfully suggest you heed his warning."

Anyon said, "Tell us."

"We need to be there when Cylian wakes up," Sean told them. "And the General and Logan need to be with us."

Anyon asked, "Why so many?"

"Because if I'm right, we have to alert the ruling council on Cygneus Prime," Sean replied. "And there isn't a moment to lose."

51

Sean hated how he was forced to return to Cylian's apartment in the company of so many others. Not to mention how Carver had already arrived with five other officials in tow. Three wore Human Assembly uniforms, the other two Sean had to assume were from Cygneus Prime. The fact they had been ghost-walked to Serena without explanation did nothing to improve their mood.

They came to full alert at Anyon's appearance. The eldest of the Human Assembly group exclaimed, "Ambassador, excellent. This ensign has the audacity to claim—"

"Hold that thought," Anyon ordered. He said to Sean, "Who should be with us?"

"But Ambassador, the Cygnean council has expressly—"

"Silence."

One of the Cygnean officials barked, "General, what is the meaning—"

"Quiet." She kept her gaze leveled on Sean and Anyon. "Proceed."

Anyon demanded, "Well?"

"We need to try to speak with Cylian," Sean replied. "All of us should be included. If they'll keep quiet."

Anyon waited while Carver translated for Brodwyn and Logan and the pair of Cygnean officials, then he addressed the entire group. "The first person to utter a sound will be summarily dismissed. Is that clear?" When his words were greeted with a stunned silence, he turned back to Sean. "Carry on."

※※※

Whatever Sandrine thought of so many people invading her sickroom, she kept to herself. When Sean asked, she replied, "There has been no change."

"Has Cylian spoken?"

"Not a word." She glanced at the figure in the bed. "Her vitals are strong, and she seems more comfortable than earlier. But she remains asleep."

Sean waited while Anyon and Carver positioned the group in a line along the side and back walls. Then he knelt by the bed and stroked Cylian's cheek. "I really, really need you to wake up."

※※※

They waited through a period long enough for the entire group to become restive. Sean did his best to ignore the shifting and muttering, but was grateful when Brodwyn finally hissed them to frozen silence. Which was when he had the idea to condense all his elemental force into the core of his being and reach out. No words, just the emotions he was feeling. Worry. Concern. Caring. Urgency.

Hope. For them.

Cylian might as well have been waiting all this time for him to signal as he did. She sighed and opened her eyes.

He cradled her face with his hands. Her eyes were luminous even when disoriented.

She coughed and touched her tongue to dry lips. Sandrine was there with a cup. Sean helped Cylian rise up far enough to drink. When she was through and had settled back, she asked softly, "Are you really here?"

"I am."

"I'm not dreaming?"

"Not just now."

"I've had the most horrid nightmares."

Sean kept stroking her face. "Will you tell me about them?"

Her eyes clouded. "They scare me."

"I know. But I think . . . Cylian, I wouldn't ask if I didn't have to. But I think talking it through could save a lot of lives."

Cylian released a pair of tears. "How do you know about them, Sean?"

"I hunted, you know, like a Watcher. They . . ."

"Scared you too."

"So much."

"How did you get away?"

Sean hesitated, not wanting to tell her anything but the truth.

"They're still hunting me, Sean." Another tear escaped. "I need to know."

Sean leaned in close enough to taste the fear in her breath. "You're safe now."

"Am I really?"

"I'm ninety-nine percent certain. I don't want to say more because I need to hear about what you saw and heard without my own experiences influencing the memories of your . . ."

"Nightmare."

"Can I ask you some questions?"

She glanced over but seemed to find nothing odd in the cluster of people watching them. "Help me up."

Sandrine helped him lift Cylian and settle pillows behind her back. She then asked for more water. When she finished drinking, she said, "Hold my hand."

"Gladly." Sean seated himself on the side of the bed. "Did you see them?"

"Just the cloud," Cylian replied. "And the light. And the fire."

"The light," Sean said. "Can you describe it?"

"A beacon. It moved. Like it was hunting me." She must have seen something in his features, because she said, "You saw it too."

"Yes." He pressed her hand, willing her not to ask more. She remained silent, her gaze steady on his. "Sandrine has heard you speak words from a tongue she does not recognize. Do you remember anything they said?"

"They did not speak. They screamed." She shivered. "One thing I remember. They shrieked it over and over and over."

"Repeat what you can."

She spoke a few words, her voice turned harsher by the recollection. A cross between a whisper and a shrill cry, elongating her jaw and tightening her neck until the veins stood out.

In response, Brodwyn's entire group gasped as one.

Anyon demanded, "What is it?"

"Old speech," Brodwyn replied. "A few remote clans still use it. Not many."

Logan said, "Some claim it was the original language of Cygneus Prime."

Brodwyn asked him, "How did you come to learn it?"

"My father tutored me in Hawk lore and this speech. He said . . ." Logan seemed to realize they had broken the enforced silence and finished with, "Sorry."

Cylian seemed genuinely interested, so Sean said, "Go on."

"My father called it the dragon tongue, a language of force and of fire. He said our greatest legacies of victory and triumph were all tied to it," Logan replied.

Anyon asked, "Can either of you translate what the lady has spoken?"

"My own study was at the Academy." Brodwyn frowned in concentration. "'The rope is loosed'?" she guessed.

"Chains," Logan said. "'The chains of old are broken. We are free once more.'"

Sean rose to his feet and faced Anyon. "Ambassador, I respectfully request that you call out the Praetorian Guard."

Anyon almost managed to repress his frown. "How many do you think we might need?"

"All of them," Sean replied. "Immediately. We might already be too late."

52

Sean's urgency was rewarded with two days of sitting on his hands. Which left him plenty of time to worry that he had gotten everything else wrong as well.

The frantic activity that captured almost everyone swept past and left him feeling not just isolated but extremely foolish.

He remained officially stationed on Aldwyn at Logan's request. The first day, he visited Cylian several times. The dreams continued to plague her, but far less than before. He said nothing about what was happening back on Cygneus Prime, and Cylian did not ask any questions.

That evening he realized that she was quite possibly a dangerous distraction. It wasn't that he might miss the action, if or when it ever came. The same ensign who had been stationed in Cylian's apartment now served as his very own personal alert system. He recorded his every transit with her before proceeding. But his focus was not on the main battle. He was exhausted—so tired his bones ached. He wanted a week off. He wanted to go somewhere special with Cylian, pull up the drawbridge, and forget the rest of the galaxy even existed. But just then he needed to take aim and hunt out everything he might have forgotten. When he kissed her goodbye, Sean thought he could see in her gaze that she knew of his change in direction. But all she said was for him to take care.

Dillon was back at the Academy, helping Carver and his superiors prepare a strategy for what Sean thought was coming. Watchers were now stationed on high orbit over Cygneus Prime. They were ordered to refrain from all bodiless hunts. They were there to survey the planet in a highly limited fashion, nothing more. The same vessel also contained a frontline bevy of Praetorians, along with the senior officers under Commander Taunton, the Praetorian who had saved Sean and Dillon from incarceration.

All discussions between the Cygnean rulers and representatives of the Human Assembly took place in the vessel's main ready room. What the Cygnean high council thought of Sean's warning and the subsequent hoopla, Sean had no idea.

No transiter had set foot on the main planet since Sean had raised the alert. Anyon had issued that order over Sean's objections. After all, Logan's team had ghost-walked for years. It was the Watchers and their hunting system that had awoken the threat. But Anyon had not been in any mood to discuss the matter, and the order remained in place.

That evening Sean returned to Aldwyn to stand duty as they laid Sidra to rest with full military honors. Logan's uncle Linux attended with two of his senior aides. The chief of the

Hawk clan was clearly cowed by how the senior Cygnean commanders treated Logan as one of their own. Tiko was there as well, because Brodwyn had ordered him and his elders to attend.

Following the funeral, Brodwyn summoned the troops to an awards ceremony. There she pinned on Logan the Cygnean medal for valor. She then promoted him to full colonel and appointed him military governor of the Outer Rim. At some point in the near future, the Cygnean council would officially declare planetary elections and Aldwyn would revert to civilian rule. Until then, Brodwyn declared in her firmest official voice, Logan's word was law.

A banquet followed the two ceremonies. Logan asked his two newly brevetted captains, Nicolette and Vance, to serve as official hosts. Following the initial toasts, Brodwyn promoted Logan's entire crew and hung medals on everyone. She and one of Anyon's ensigns then transited back to the vessel stationed over Cygneus Prime. As the party grew both loud and raucous, Sean transited to the vessel as well, to ensure there had been no change to the planet's calm. Then he retreated to his newly assigned quarters in the Aldwyn militia headquarters.

After the banquet, Logan stopped by Sean's room and complained bitterly over Tiko being allowed to go free. Sean said nothing and let the newly brevetted colonel vent. The loss of Sidra clearly lay heavy on Logan's heart. But Sean thought Brodwyn was probably right to keep Tiko in place, at least for the moment. Linux and the Hawks might have come out on top, but Clan Havoc was going nowhere. At least this way, the Havoc fief was ruled by someone firmly under Logan's thumb.

The next morning, Sean's ensign woke him with the news that Ambassador Anyon awaited him in the mess hall. Sean showered and dressed and found the Diplomat listening intently as Vance, Nicolette, and Logan designed a strategy on a tabletop using plates, spoons, mugs, and lines of engagement drawn with cold coffee.

When Sean approached, Anyon excused himself and asked, "Do you need something to eat?"

"Just coffee."

"Grab yourself a mug, and let us depart. There's something I think you should see."

※ ※ ※

The inland sea of what formerly had been the Hawk fief was gripped by a frigid winter wind. Anyon sent the ensign for warm coats, then motioned for Sean to walk the beach with him. Sean did not mind the bitter cold. He was outdoors, breathing real air, filled with scents and seasons and life.

A series of tree-covered islands was strung along the shore like an icy necklace. Beyond that was nothing save white-capped waves and a shore lost to mist and distance. Some of the islands he could see were little more than rocky mounds, covered with an impenetrable tangle of brambles and wind-scarred trees. The one where they walked was vast by comparison, at least a couple of miles from end to end, and shaped like a crescent moon.

When the ensign returned with jackets, Anyon instructed

her to await them on the orbiting vessel and pointed Sean down to the rocky shoreline. As they walked the beach, Anyon pointed out the weapons that now rimmed the shore. "The Cygnean high command would not do this because I insisted, or even because General Brodwyn ordered. They did it because they agree with your assessment."

Sean released a breath he'd been holding since issuing his warning. "What if I got it wrong?"

"Then you did it for all the right reasons."

"I've been so worried," he confessed.

"I know you have, which is why we're here. So that I can tell you this: I and every other senior official have been where you now are." Anyon let that sink in for a long moment, then asked, "What led you to your conclusion?"

"It was Kaviti," Sean replied. "He was obsessed with this system. He clearly discovered the legends about the Grey Assassins and the ditrinium weapons they wielded. I realized that if one component of the planet's lore was true, the other probably was as well. Then I was attacked while I was hunting Clan Havoc, and the Watchers went berserk, and Cylian was assaulted when she dozed off in the meeting. It all pointed to just one possible conclusion."

"A conclusion no one else managed to see," Anyon added.

"What's happened to Kaviti?"

"An interplanetary arrest warrant has been issued for the Ambassador and his entire cadre. He is no doubt crouched in some dark corner where he hopes we cannot reach him. But it is only a matter of time before we apprehend him and his Assassins."

Sean had his doubts but said nothing.

They walked in silence as they passed in front of a pair of massive weapons trained at the lake's placid surface. Then Anyon said, "Becoming aware of a planetary threat is a great feat."

"If I'm right," Sean added.

Anyon waved that aside. "My daughter called you an Adept. Only time will tell if this is the case. What I can say is that you have the makings of a very gifted Diplomat. Whether or not you are correct in this one assessment will not alter my opinion. It is not because of this one conclusion that I address you as I do."

Sean's legs refused to take another step. Anyon took another couple of paces before he realized that he walked alone. He turned back and revealed a craggy smile. "Time and again you have taken what others view as a great series of disconnected shards and knit together the vessel from which they all came. You repeatedly do this in the midst of chaos and conflict. Lives depend upon a Diplomat being able to accomplish such feats, even in the fire of battle."

Sean heard his voice break as he asked, "What if I got this all wrong?"

"Sooner or later in your career, you will do just that. You will shame yourself and everyone who has trusted you by making a monumentally bad decision." The Ambassador turned and stared out to sea. "The wrong verdicts will haunt you, as they do me. You will carry them as lifelong burdens."

Sean had no idea what to say.

"That is the cost of holding the sort of power and responsibility that form the Diplomat's life. And the fact that you are burdened by these uncertainties is an indication that I am right to speak with you as I do." His gaze swiveled around to fasten upon Sean, holding a force as fierce and implacable as the winter storm that surrounded them. "Such elements cannot be taught. They are gifts. And such gifts as these can only be honed."

"Your daughter once said you were the most intelligent of men. I think she was right," Sean said.

Anyon drew himself up to full height. "I want you to become a senior aide on my staff."

"I accept," Sean replied hoarsely.

"Excellent. You will attend classes in the school of Diplomacy. We will meet on occasion, but I do not care to involve you in mundane duties at present. Instead, your appointment will remain confidential between us and the head of the school. I will personally ask her to serve as your tutor."

"Sir . . . Thank you."

"You are most welcome. It is well deserved." Anyon glanced at his timepiece. "Now unless there is something else, I suggest—"

Anyon did not have an opportunity to finish his question. Which was probably for the best, because Sean had been about to ask if he would be required to serve with Elenya. But all that was suddenly shoved aside.

The winter lake turned molten. Then the shoreline was blasted by fire.

53

Flames rising from the lake formed a roiling wave, a tsunami of rage. Steam blasted in a funnel straight into the air. Mist billowed out from this central pillar like a giant wheel. A wave of fire rose up and descended upon the shore where they stood. Sean had time to register all this in the one brief instant it took to grip the Ambassador's arms and step away.

As it was, they were almost too late.

They landed on the orbiting vessel and sprawled in the foyer that served as the ready room for the flight deck and the Cygnean council chamber. Thankfully, Brodwyn was there, deep in conversation with Commander Taunton. A meeting must have just broken up, because the antechamber held a dozen or so people. They all gaped in shock at the sight of the two new arrivals. Both Sean and Anyon smoldered from the flames that had almost consumed them.

Sean croaked, "It's happening."

Brodwyn used her parade-ground voice to command, "Sound the alarm!"

As Sean helped Anyon rise to his feet, the Ambassador showed his age for the very first time. Being that close to his own death had clearly left him shattered. He gripped Sean's arm with tremulous force and whispered, "You saved my life."

Sean saw Brodwyn gesture to him and knew the Ambassador's comments would have to wait. "Sir, I need to go back."

Anyon's gaze searched the metal chamber for a fury that was not there. "Back?"

Sean gently pried away Anyon's fingers and said what the Ambassador needed to hear. "You're safe now."

Brodwyn reached out as Sean approached. "Show me."

* * *

Sean, Brodwyn, and Commander Taunton returned with the first contingent of Praetorian Guards. A frontline phalanx had been stationed on the orbiting vessel to serve as shock troops. The shipboard Watchers were backed up by ground troops on observation detail with direct comm links to the vessel. The reason for their silence was clear the instant they arrived back on Cygneus Prime.

The forward command post was atop a trio of steel towers built upon a hill overlooking the eastern cannons. Or it would have been, if the blasters still existed. The first waves of flames had rolled back by the time they arrived, leaving behind a sea rimmed by ash and heaps of molten metal.

The Praetorians transited onto transport platforms that

looked to Sean like floating patios. More and more of the transports lifted from the ground and hovered over the blackened earth. The lake boiled, and the rising steam clouds were fierce enough to defy the winter storm. Sean felt his face sweat and his back freeze.

Brodwyn was busy regrouping her ground troops when Carver appeared at the tower's rear quarter. He stepped forward and saluted Brodwyn. "General, I suggest—"

His comment was cut off by the second assault, which caused even these hardened warriors to freeze in shock.

54

To Sean, the beasts most resembled giant moray eels. Ones that blasted fire. Their bodies were brown as dried earth and mottled with darker splotches. They were thick as freight trains and just as long. The first three to fully emerge wriggled through the ash and took snakelike aim at the tower where they stood.

Sean screamed with half a dozen others, "*Shields!*"

An instant later, flames engulfed their platforms.

The beasts were *fast*.

In less than half a dozen frantic heartbeats, a dragon wrapped itself around their tower and blanketed them with the stench of seaweed and dead fish. The tower was protected with the same force that kept them alive. But with a series of loud bangs, the beast wrenched away the structure's foundations.

Brodwyn gripped Sean's arm and shouted loud enough for all the tower's occupants to hear, "Overhead platform! Go!"

They transited up and crowded the railing. Directly below, the tower was now freed from its shield and was instantly crushed to a single twisted scrap. The fiend released its hold, sought a new prey, spotted the platform, and blasted them yet again.

Their pilot shifted position away from the flames, granting them a bird's-eye view of more and more eels emerging from the waters. The lake's surface boiled now, a single writhing mass of elongated, fire-breathing worms.

Brodwyn gripped her comm link with a fierceness that turned her hands to talons. "Team one, cage the sea! Team two, enfold and trap!"

The Praetorians were organized into the same tight units that had bested the aliens' latest invasion. The downside was communication. Organizing their reprisal meant directing several hundred cadres. Commander Taunton took control of the seabound forces, with Carver and Dillon serving as his seconds. Brodwyn directed the assault upon the nine beasts that were advancing across the shore toward her troops' rear positions.

Gradually their tactics developed into a sense of control and order. The beasts' forward momentum became glutinous, as though they were trapped in invisible cages. But their immense fury did not diminish. Even when their progress was halted, they continued to shoot out great bouts of flame. Then nooses formed by the Praetorians' combined force were fitted around the nine snouts, and the fires were extinguished.

Smoke and flames blasted across the sea's surface, illuminating the multitude of cages that now enveloped all the remaining beasts.

One of Brodwyn's rear guards shot a cannonade at the nearest sea cage. A faint crack appeared in the shield, and a head wriggled free and spouted fire at the closest transports.

"Cease fire! Cease fire!" Brodwyn was genuinely irate. "Who released that shot?"

Wisely, the comm link gave off nothing but a faint static.

"The next idiot who fires I will personally skin alive!" Brodwyn watched as the Praetorians crammed the beast's head back inside and rebuilt the shield. She then said to Taunton, "With your permission, Commander, we will move on to the next step."

In reply, Taunton said into his comm link, "Begin phase three."

55

The eels that had emerged farthest from the ash rimming the inland sea were stretched out taut. Their quarter-mile lengths were trapped within a multitude of Praetorian shields. Even so, their bodies continually spasmed in furious efforts to break free. Every tight breath shot puffs of flame across the fields by their heads.

Brodwyn said, "Proceed, Commander."

Taunton said into his comm link, "On my signal. One, two, three, *lift!*"

Nine snared mouths snarled in futile rage as the beasts were raised from the ground. Dozens of transport pods surrounded them on every side—up, down, sides, front, and back. They made a bizarre yet stately procession as they crossed snow-dappled fields, a string of low hills, and a grove of winter-bare trees. The entire journey was punctuated by snarls and tight flame bursts. Sean's platform held the lead position. When he looked back, he saw lips rippling with fury, revealing teeth as long as he was tall.

Their destination was a lake nestled deep within a steep, snow-covered valley. Sean had only seen pictures up to that point. He thought the setting was almost perfect. The lake was about half a mile wide, and its placid surface reflected the slate-grey sky.

Dillon spoke for the first time since the attack began. "This place is a beaut. Shame we've got to mess it up."

Sean did not realize his brother had spoken in English until Brodwyn demanded, "What did he say?"

She gave a terse nod at Sean's translation, then told Taunton, "Position the beasts, Commander."

"Aye, ma'am." At his orders, the nine fiends were stationed like writhing arrows around the lake's outer perimeter. Their snouts were angled down, down, down to the lake. "They are all in place, General."

"Give the order, Commander."

He leaned forward so as to direct his smile at Sean. "It was the young man's idea, General. Perhaps he should have the honor."

Brodwyn ordered, "All transports are to move back behind the safety perimeter."

They left the eels alone and reversed back another hundred meters.

Taunton said, "All transports in position, General."

She handed the comm link to Sean. "Call it in."

Sean exchanged an excited grin with his brother, then said, "Drop the bomb."

56

The bomb was large enough to require a transport of its own. The transport was shaped like a metal crab, with multiple limbs for scooping and maneuvering heavy loads. It hovered directly over the center of the icebound lake and released its solitary load.

The bomb descended silently through the air, pierced the lake's icy surface, and disappeared with a soft splash.

For a long moment, the only sound was the gasping snarls from the captured beasts.

Then the bomb ignited.

The platforms and monsters were all shielded from the blast. Even so, the force was powerful enough to shake their vision. When the mist and roar and smoke subsided, the lake was just . . .

Gone.

For the first time since their assault began, the monsters were completely, utterly . . .

Still.

The valley was blasted clean of snow, grass, trees, shrubs, water. The former lake was nothing more than a deep pit in the earth.

Brodwyn turned to Logan and said, "Would you be so good as to translate?"

"It would be an honor, General."

She said into her comm link, "Full amplification." Then she handed it over and began, "We were not the ones to attack your stronghold. We seek only peace between our races—" She stopped because Logan shook his head. "Yes?"

"General, the dragon speech has no word for 'peace.'"

"Is that so?"

"My father took great pride in the fact."

"As I fear did too many others of our forebears. Very well. Tell them, 'We seek an end to war.'" She waited as he translated, then continued, "If you ever attack us again, we will annihilate your entire race. But so long as you do not attack, then the inland sea will remain your abode. What is more, we will do our utmost to keep you safe. We would ask for an alliance between our races. There is no doubt much we could learn from you. But that is for you to decide. If you wish to communicate with us, you should make contact with our . . ." She turned to Logan. "Do they have a word for the ghost-walkers who hunt?"

"Aye, ma'am."

When he was done, she went on, "You may continue to search the hidden space beyond your realm. But so shall we. This point is not negotiable. And know this. Any attack, any assault on one of our ghost-walkers, and your entire race will be no more. This is the only warning you will ever receive." She gave that a moment, then finished, "Break this code at your peril."

When Logan had finished translating, she retrieved the comm link and said, "Return these fiends to their waters."

57

ine days later, Sean stood in the Cygnean government's main audience chamber. Sweating bullets.

The government palace sat atop the tallest hill in the capital city's heart. Beyond windows draped in royal purple spread a civilization in all its mystery. Sean could not have cared less.

He had wanted another month, but Anyon had refused his request and Brodwyn had agreed with him. Sean suspected both leaders knew he had been hoping to avoid this altogether. Which was probably why they had been so adamant that he show up today.

There was also the small matter of how the Cygnean ruling council was growing increasingly impatient to hear his report.

While Sean paced the outer foyer, Dillon was already inside the ruling council's chamber next door. Carver and Taunton were also inside, reporting on the interstellar hunt for Kaviti, his Assassins, and the ditrinium blades. There was nothing they could do about the technology. It was outlawed now, and everything about it was classified as top secret. But Kaviti was still out there, and Sean thought the threat it represented to all transiters was probably permanent. Another item Sean's former professor had to answer for, when the Praetorians caught up with him.

All of Kaviti's former allies in the Human Assembly had disavowed him, of course. They called him a rogue, a fool, and far worse besides. The cadre and their broader coalition were in full retreat. And their idiotic concepts had been publicly denounced.

As Dillon put it, the result wasn't as satisfying as seeing them all sentenced to life without parole. But it would have to do.

Logan was there in the antechamber, along with Vance and Nicolette. They were scheduled to enter with Sean. That had been Brodwyn's idea. As though extra manpower would help calm his nerves.

Truth be told, it was far better than facing the rulers of an alien system alone.

Sean's past nine days had been spent poring over Kaviti's private journals, piecing together his forty-year research into the history of Cygneus Prime. There had been serious objections at first. When Anyon faced opposition from the Institute's pompous faculty, he took up the matter before the entire Assembly, who passed a resolution appointing Sean as temporary custodian of all Kaviti's effects, including his offices and staff at the Institute.

And the Judiciary.

And the Assembly.

From prisoner to potentate in one fell swoop.

The young ensign who had camped out in Cylian's front room now served as Sean's personal aide. Each morning she presented Sean with piles of invitations from half a dozen worlds. Apparently people assumed he was now someone important enough to know.

Sean ignored it all and busied himself with tracking through four decades of research. Thankfully, Kaviti had kept precise notes. His journals dated back to his first assignment as a junior Counselor, which had been to the outpost region that contained the Cygnean system.

It all came down to the dragons.

Only two worlds within the Human Assembly had fought pitched battles against such beasts—Serena, in its far distant past, and Cygneus Prime. If ever the beasts agreed to talk with them, that was the issue Sean intended to focus upon. Had they once transited between worlds? It seemed obvious they had, as transiting was the natural component to the Watchers' ability to hunt, which the dragons clearly shared. Was it the Ancients who had confined them? That was another issue Sean wanted to raise. And if so, why on these two worlds?

For the moment, the one thing Sean could definitely say was that the Cygnean love of combat had destroyed the earliest records. From the dawn of humanity, Cygneus Prime had been home to warlords and battle. Whatever treaty the monsters had referred to in their communication through Cylian's nightmares was lost. But Sean suspected everything that had come out these last days—the ditrinium and the weapons and the methods of fighting—had their start in this battle between man and beast.

Which meant Kaviti had ferreted his way through fragments and snippets and rumors and legends.

No wonder the man had been obsessed.

***

Cylian was seated in a gilded chair beneath a tapestry the size of a putting green. The artwork depicted some long-ago battle. Of course.

She was doing much better but still tired easily. Sean turned from the windows and walked over. "Are you all right?"

"I'm fine, Sean. Thanks to you." She studied him a moment, then replied, "I'm the one who should be asking you that."

He glanced at the ornately carved doors leading to the council chambers. "Definitely not."

"You're going to do great."

Sean pretended to study the two guards in official dress uniforms that flanked the portal.

"Sean."

"What?"

"I know what's troubling you." When he did not respond, Cylian said it for him. "Elenya is in there. Seated next to her father."

Sean slumped into the chair next to hers. "This is awful."

"Did it ever occur to you that Anyon set this up precisely as it is?"

Sean turned in his seat. Despite Cylian's pale exterior and the plum-colored circles under her eyes, her beauty shone through. "No."

"That's what I think. Commander Taunton does as well."

"You discussed my ex-girlfriend with the Praetorian commander?"

"He asked what troubled you. I replied."

Sean realized, "You're enjoying this."

"Well, perhaps a little." She reached for his hand. "Do you know what is the hardest thing for a strong person to do?"

He was tempted to reply with, *I'm not strong. You are.* But he merely said, "What?"

"Admit to weakness," Cylian replied. "And ask for help. You have been strong for me through the hardest days and nights of my life thus far. You've served as the wise planner whose work has saved thousands of lives. More. Now I want you to look around this room, my darling."

"You've never called me that before," Sean said.

"Look," she softly repeated. When he did so, she went on, "All these people are here because of you. And they want nothing more than to support you. To praise you."

He released a fraction of his tension. "I'm scared."

"Your former girlfriend unsettles you. It is perfectly understandable." Cylian leaned close enough for him to feel her breath upon his cheek. "But here is a secret, my darling. Elenya is part of your past. I am part of your future."

The guards snapped to attention as the portals opened and Brodwyn stepped into the audience hall. She smiled at Sean and said, "Are you ready?"

Sean felt warm fingers tighten briefly, then release his hand. He rose to his feet. "Yes."

Thomas Locke is a pseudonym for Davis Bunn, the award-winning novelist with worldwide sales of seven million copies in twenty-five languages. Davis divides his time between Oxford and Florida and holds a lifelong passion for speculative stories. He is the author of *Emissary* and *Merchant of Alyss* in the Legends of the Realm series, as well as *Fault Lines*, *Trial Run*, and *Flash Point* in the Fault Lines series. Learn more at www.tlocke.com.

Don't miss a moment
in the explosive
FAULT LINES
series!

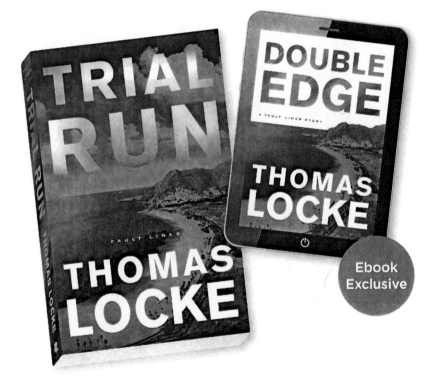

Ebook Exclusive

In the clash of science, government, and big business,
one thing remains clear: **what you don't know can kill you.**

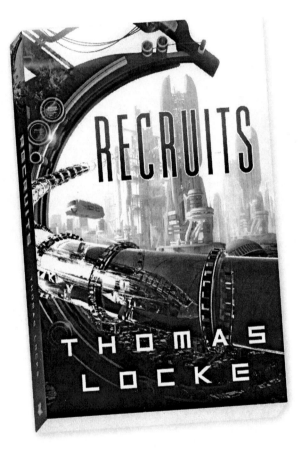

"Carr's debut, the first in a series, is assured and up-tempo, with much to enjoy in characterization and description."

—*Publishers Weekly*

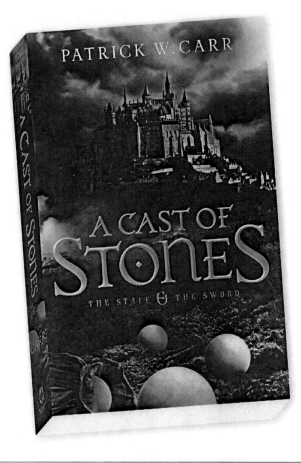

Drunkard Errol Stone has to shape up fast when his hunt for the next glass unwittingly merges with a dangerous quest to save his kingdom.

BETHANYHOUSE
a division of Baker Publishing Group
www.BethanyHouse.com

Available wherever books and ebooks are sold.

THEIR BATTLE FOR THE THRONE HAS JUST BEGUN.
But Will It Matter If the World They Rule Collapses into the Sea?

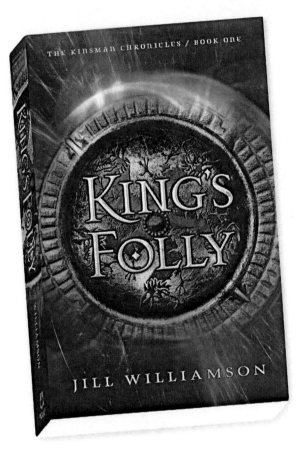

Prince Wilek's father believes the disasters plaguing their land signal impending doom, but Wilek thinks this is superstitious nonsense—until he is sent to investigate a fresh calamity. What he discovers is more cataclysmic than he could've imagined. Wilek sets out on a desperate quest to save his people, but can he succeed before the entire land crumbles?

Be the First to Hear
about Other New Books
from REVELL!

Sign up for announcements about
new and upcoming titles at

RevellBooks.com/SignUp

Don't miss out on our great reads!

Revell

a division of Baker Publishing Group
www.RevellBooks.com